Walter von der Vogelweide

Selected Poems of Walter von der Vogelweide

The Minnesinger

Walter von der Vogelweide

Selected Poems of Walter von der Vogelweide
The Minnesinger

ISBN/EAN: 9783743377950

Manufactured in Europe, USA, Canada, Australia, Japa

Cover: Foto ©Andreas Hilbeck / pixelio.de

Manufactured and distributed by brebook publishing software (www.brebook.com)

Walter von der Vogelweide

Selected Poems of Walter von der Vogelweide

ELECTED POEMS

OF

W   VON DER VOGELW

THE MINNESINGER

DONE INTO ENGLISH VERSE

INTRODUCTION AND SIX ILLUSTRAT

BY

ER ALISON PHILLIPS, M.A.

LATE SCHOLAR OF MERTON COLLEGE

SCHOLAR OF ST. JOHN'S COLLEGE, OXFOR

LONDON

SMITH, ELDER, & CO., 15 WATERLOO

1896

PREFACE

THE name of Walter von der Vogelweide is, even in England, not entirely unknown. Longfellow has told again the charming legend of the poet leaving a provision in his will for the birds to be fed daily at his tomb for ever ; and the many admirers of Wagner will remember Walter von Stolzing's song in the ' Meistersänger '—

> Herr Walter von der Vogelweide,
> 'Twas he that taught me singing !

and that in the opera of ' Tannhäuser' he appears among the minstrels who take part in the contest at the Wartburg.

In Germany, however, the name of the greatest of the Minnesingers has, after an oblivion of many centuries, once again become almost a household word ; and this not only because the awakened national consciousness of the German people has been glad to gather up the threads of connection with its brighter past, but because the new enthusiasm aroused by the patriotic movement which culminated in the events of 1870 produced a demand for a patriotic poetry, of which Walter was so admirable a master.

Of the two greatest names of modern German literature, Goethe had from the first been accused of want of patriotism, while Heine's French sympathies have put him, as it were, under the ban of the New Empire.

Walter's stirring rhymes, then, whether read in the original Middle High German, or in Simrock's excellent translation, have served in a certain measure to fill a void, and to inspire in the nineteenth, as in the thirteenth century, a certain number of imitators.

This would, perhaps, be sufficient excuse for offering an English translation to the public. But, apart from his revived popularity in Germany, Walter von der Vogelweide should appeal in England to very various tastes and interests ; and I have some hope that this translation may prove useful not only to students and lovers of literature, but also, and perhaps more especially, to historians, who may not have access to his writings in the original.

In making the translations, I have endeavoured to keep closely to the original, in form and metre as well as in spirit, though the completely different genius of modern English and mediæval German has, as will be readily understood, made an exact reproduction unattainable.

PREFACE

I have based these translations, in the main, on Pfeiffer's edition of Walter von der Vogelweide (revised by Karl Bartsch : Leipzig, Brockhaus, 6th. ed. 1880) ; but several poems which he rejects as not genuine, notably the beautiful 'May Song,' I have included on the authority of Lachmann, whose edition of the text remains the standard one, and who is followed by Simrock. For the Introduction and notes I have used, besides Pfeiffer and Simrock, the very interesting monograph on Walter von der Vogelweide and his poems by Herr Wilmanns ('Walther von der Vogelweide und seine Zeit.' Bonn, 1882). Scherer's 'History of German Literature' (translated by Mrs. Conybeare : Oxford, Clar. Press, 1886) gives a very clear account of the literature of the period. For the general history of the times Raumer's 'Geschichte der Hohenstaufen' will be found an inexhaustible mine of information.

WALTER ALISON PHILLIPS.

CONTENTS

CONTENTS

CONTENTS

POLITICAL POEMS

CONTENTS

LIST OF ILLUSTRATIONS

———

INTRODUCTION

———•∞•———

IN the poetry of Walter von der Vogelweide the qualities
which most impress those who read it for the first time are
a certain perennial freshness breathing through it, and the
broadly human standpoint from which it is written, by
virtue of which, though composed in an age so remote
from our own, it appeals very directly to modern taste and
sentiment.

This power of freeing itself from the fetters imposed
by contemporary fashion and convention is always one of
the distinguishing marks of true genius. Yet, since no
originality, however marked, can entirely cut itself off from
the influence of its environment, it is essential to the proper
understanding of the great poets of the past that we should
have some knowledge of the conditions under which they
lived and worked. And of Walter von der Vogelweide this
is especially true. For he, in a manner far more vivid than
any of his contemporaries, reflects the character and thought,
the ideals and aims, of a period of singular interest in the
history of the world.

Born about the year 1170, of poor but not ignoble parentage, Walter's lot was cast in an epoch of great men and great ideas. It was the age of Innocent III., in whose person the power and pretensions of the Papacy reached their zenith; of Frederick I., whose dream was the restoration of the empire of Charlemagne and the universal dominion of the Cæsars; of Henry VI. and Frederick II., under whom the dream was, once and again, all but realised. Nor were these manifestations of the working of a new vitality among the nations of Europe confined to the splendid ambitions of a few select and masterful spirits. All Western Christendom seemed astir with a new and hitherto hidden and undeveloped energy, pregnant with great results for religion, for art, for literature, and for the polity of nations.

Into the causes of this "Mediæval Renaissance" it is unnecessary to enter at length. Something was doubtless due to the influence of the Crusades, resulting as they did in a closer contact with the culture of the East; something perhaps to the reaction which followed the fateful year 1000, long fixed upon by the superstition of the dark ages as the final term of the world, and the consequent awakening in the minds of the people of a new sense of the value of life, and a new inducement to effort.

Whatever were the causes of this intellectual revival, its

effects were first felt in Provence and the south of France. Here indeed the traditions of ancient culture, though grown dim and half mythical, had never wholly perished ; and here, among an imaginative and impressionable people, the seeds of any fresh external influence would fall upon a fertile soil. France[1] thus became the focus of the new movement, and, though the throne of Charlemagne had been transferred to the more barbarous North, her empire over men's minds and manners was more complete than ever, and in all questions, religious, social, and intellectual, her influence in Europe was paramount. Nor, indeed, could the results of her rich and varied activity fail to produce an overpowering effect upon the imagination of less cultured neighbours. Most of the great ecclesiastics of the eleventh and twelfth centuries were, by birth or domicile, Frenchmen ; it is sufficient to mention the names of Lanfranc, Anselm, Suger, and Bernard of Clairvaux. It was the genius of Frenchmen which, during the same period, was gradually building up, out of the ruins of the ancient world, the glorious structure of Gothic architecture ; it was the imagination of Frenchmen which evolved that system of chivalry which had so profound and civilising an effect on the society of the middle ages ;

---

[1] I use the term France for the sake of convenience, but, of course, not in its modern sense of a homogeneous nation.

and, lastly, it was through France that Europe was made
acquainted with the gay and joyous poetry which, under
the influence of such fragments as still survived of classical
literature, had been the creation of the troubadours of
Provence.

Of all European peoples, the Germans, both from their
geographical position and from their susceptibility to
foreign influence, were most profoundly affected by the
example of France. The tendency of the upper classes in
Germany to imitate French dress and manners, which had
been apparent as early as the beginning of the eleventh
century, received an additional stimulus through the
marriage, in 1043, of the Emperor, Henry III., to
Agnes of Poitiers. From this period onward, throughout
the twelfth century, the influence of France was continually
on the increase. It showed itself in every department of
life ; in games, in sport, in costume, in art. The 'simplicity
of old German manners' was stigmatised as 'boorish,'
and the rules of the new courtesy became part of the
education of every aspirant to knighthood. In literature,
too, as well as in social customs, the overpowering influence
of France determined the line of advance. The chivalrous
epics of this period, which superseded the older German
religious and popular poetry, were, for the most part,
merely free transcriptions of French originals. Even the

most characteristic of all German national epics, the Nibelungenlied, had been remodelled to suit the prevailing taste, and the rugged outlines of the old saga filled in with the somewhat tawdry and stippled colouring of the new chivalrous romances.[1]

In the same manner, the love poetry which the French had learned from the troubadours of Provence was by them in turn handed on to their German neighbours; and just as the French epics, taking root in German soil, had budded into a new and more vigorous growth, so, in the hands of the Minnesingers, the love songs of the troubadours gradually acquired a new character and depth.

That this poetry, developed on its own lines, could ever have attained to any real excellence as a means of expressing human emotion was impossible in the narrow and highly artificial conditions under which it was evolved. For it was the creation of the new chivalry, with its complex social relations, and at every step was shackled by rules, by conventions, and by the prejudices of a society split up into numerous sharply defined castes. The songs then are, for the most part, as artificial as the society in

---

[1] Carl Lachmann, the great scholar to whose patience and critical insight it is mainly due that modern Germany has regained the works of her mediæval poets, has attempted, in his edition of the Nibelungenlied, to sift the earlier form of the epic from the matter added later, which he prints in separate type.

which they were produced. They deal in general with but
one theme—love ; and this, the most untameable of human
passions, was, owing to the exigencies of social custom,
confined and fettered in its poetic expression by every
sort of restriction. It was, in the first place, a conceit of
the new culture that love was too noble a theme to be
entrusted to any but men of noble birth. The wandering
gleemen, who catered for the vulgar herd, must confine
themselves to popular romances or didactic poems :

> He who begs for cast-off clothes
> Unworthy is to sing of love.

The poetry of love became, then, the prerogative of a
class. But, more than this, the many gradations of rank
and dignity among the nobly born gave but little scope for
that free and unfettered intercourse which alone would
have fostered the true and natural growth of the chivalrous
poetry. For the professional minstrels of knightly rank,
who had arisen to supply the demands of fashion, were
too much akin to the despised class of wandering
gleemen to meet with anything better than a half con-
temptuous toleration in the noble circles they served to
amuse.

They were, in fact, like Walter von der Vogelweide,
generally the sons of poor and humble retainers of the
great feudal chiefs, and depended entirely on their art for

their daily bread. As the gleemen wandered from tavern
to tavern, so the minstrels travelled from court to court,
happy if they were retained for a while among the train of
a prince more generous than usual ; and forced, as Walter
bitterly complains, to receive, with the humblest of bows,
the largess which their patron might choose to bestow.
Yet, by the conventions of their art, they were compelled
to select in this proud and exclusive circle the mistress to
whom they addressed their song.

Under these circumstances, there was no question of
a deep and true poetry of love ; and in the poems of
most of the Minnesingers the passion of love, in its
best modern sense, has little place. For them the reward of faithful service was not that union, perfect till
death, which is the ideal of a less artificial society, but
stolen interviews and unlawful kisses. Between the
humble singer and his highborn 'Lady' there could
be no thought of marriage ; and, indeed, in a society
where unmarried girls were kept in great seclusion, the
ladies to whom the poets addressed their songs were,
more often than not, already wives. And from this it followed that, by another convention, the identity of the lady
to whom a poet was supposed to be paying his addresses
had to be kept by him a profound secret ; and so we find,
in the love poems of the troubadours and their pupils, very

little 'local colouring,' and everything connected with their
mistress described in the most general terms, lest perchance
the veil should be torn aside, and both the lady and the
singer disgraced. Yet even this immoral tone of the
mediæval love poetry was a mere convention. It was,
like the typical modern French novel, the creation of a
social system in which pure romance was rendered almost
impossible by the marriage customs of the time. For, as
has been very justly pointed out, it is impossible to suppose
that, even if the 'gallant troubadours' had escaped the
vigilance of the 'watchers' or 'guardians' of whom they so
often complain, the fathers, husbands, and brothers of the
ladies in question would have for a moment tolerated the
presence of the low-born singers,[1] much less rewarded
them, if their poetical hopes and aspirations had been
taken seriously.

Such, then, was the tradition which the Minnesingers
had received from the troubadours, and to which they had
in the main adhered—the tradition of a poetry as conventional in sentiment as it was in form. And this it is very
necessary to bear in mind, if we would understand a certain
inconsistency in the tone of some of the greater of the Minne-

---

[1] This view of the Minnesingers needs modification in so far as it would
apply only to the *professional* minstrels. There were doubtless distinguished
singers of all ranks ; and the list includes such names as the Emperors Henry
VI. and Frederick II., and the unhappy Conradin.

singers: a want of harmony between what may be called their conventional immorality, and the high ideals of right conduct which the nobler among them often inculcate. For, in fact, the light poetry of Provence had, in its progress into Germany, been touched by the more serious spirit of the North. Its conventionalities were in the main retained, as the fashion of the day dictated. There are still the old complaints of the 'watchers' and 'guardians'; the sighs for favours too long deferred; the affectation of an intimacy which had no place in fact. But, side by side with all this, there was gradually growing up a nobler view of love; a realisation of the essential difference between true and false love, of the power of a pure love to elevate the character of a man, of the necessity for self-denial and self-devotion in the lover; and gradually, too, was being evolved the portrait of the ideal woman as she appeared to the imagination of the best of the poets: the picture of a refined lady, well-bred, reserved, and modest. 'Better than all the glories of the Spring,' sings Walter von der Vogelweide, is it—

> When a noble maiden, fair and pure,
> With raiment rich, and tresses deftly braided,
>   Mingles, for pleasure's sake, in company,
> High-bred, with eyes that, laughingly demure,
> Glance round at times, and make all else seem faded —
>   As, when the sun shines, all the stars must die.

And again :

> We men maintain that constancy
> Is a good woman's highest pride ;
> If she have wit and modesty,
> 'Tis rose and lily side by side.

While, of the effect of a true love upon character, he says :

> Whoso the love of a good woman heeds
> Will be ashamed of evil deeds.

This high ideal of womanhood, and nobler view of love, Walter von der Vogelweide shared with others. For him alone was reserved the glory of freeing his song from the fetters of a narrow convention, and of proclaiming aloud, in the face of no little scorn and hostile criticism, that love was not the prerogative of a caste, but the birthright of gentle and simple alike.[1] And it is just these charming verses, with their delicately suggestive colouring, which he either addresses to or puts into the mouth of daughters of the people, that are the highest achievement of mediæval lyrical poetry.

The poetry of Provence, with its impatience of religious and moral control, as brilliant, as artificial, and as evanescent as a display of fireworks, was but the product of a people 'old and decadent before it had reached maturity ;'[2]

---

[1] See especially the poem ' Woman and Lady,' p. 59.
[2] Lavallée, quoted by Raumer, *Hohenstaufen*, vol. vi., p. 445.

and, even without the crusading hordes of Simon de
Montfort, it would have perished through its own inherent
corruption. The faults of the Minnesingers, on the other
hand, are not those of decadence, but of inexperience
and youth ; and, had Germany been spared the miseries
which followed the fall of the house of Hohenstaufen, —
Walter might have become, like Chaucer in England,
the intellectual father of a long and glorious line of
poets.

It is probable that, but for the overwhelming religious
and social cataclysm which convulsed the world at the close
of the twelfth century, Walter von der Vogelweide would
never have left the traditional paths of chivalrous poetry.
But the year 1198, which saw the death of Frederick of
Austria, the first of his patrons, marked a memorable epoch
also in the affairs of Germany and of the world, and for a
time drew the young poet from lighter themes into the
field of political and religious strife.

In September, 1197, the Emperor Henry VI., after
raising the Empire to an unprecedented height of glory,
and establishing his power up to the very gates of Rome,
had, at the early age of thirty-two, and in the mid-career
of his success, been suddenly cut off. A few months later,
in January, 1198, Celestine IV., his antagonist, also died ;
and the vacancy of the Holy See was speedily filled up by

the election of the Cardinal Lothair, who took the memorable name of Innocent III.

Never had the essential weakness of the Germanic Empire and the inherent strength of the Papacy presented such a vivid contrast. The death of the Emperor, and the uncertainty of the succession, undid in a moment the work of years ; and while the Empire, deprived of its head, lay distracted and helpless, the new Pope could take up at once the thread of policy where his predecessor had dropped it, and, under the most favourable circumstances, apply his iron will and consummate statesmanship to building up once more the fallen fortunes of the see of Peter.

The death of the Emperor was the signal for the emancipation of all those lawless and disruptive elements in the Empire which his genius had kept under control. The succession, which, had he lived a few years longer, would, in all probability, have devolved easily and naturally upon his son, afterwards the Emperor Frederick II., became the subject of a long and ruinous civil war. Frederick was at this time but three years old ; and though his father had caused him to be formally acknowledged as his successor, and though his uncle, Duke Philip of Suabia, at first proclaimed himself the protector of his nephew's interests, the prospect of a long minority was, under the circumstances of the Empire, not to be regarded without serious misgiving ; and Philip was soon forced, in the interests of the Empire, as well as of the house of Hohenstaufen, to put forward his own claims to the crown.

For, in the meantime, a strong party among the German princes, headed by the Archbishop of Cologne, had offered the crown to Otho, Count of Poitou, a nephew of Richard I. of England, and second son of the old Duke Henry the Lion of Brunswick, who, as the head of the house of Guelph, had been the most dangerous rival of the Hohenstaufen. Otho, seeing in this crisis a favourable opportunity for restoring the fortunes of his house, accepted the call, and, supported by the money and the moral influence of his uncle, Richard I., marched upon Aix-la-Chapelle, took the town by storm, and was there solemnly crowned as King of the Romans by the Archbishop of Cologne. It is unnecessary to enter into the weary struggle that followed. For years Germany was devastated by all the horrors of civil war ; and for years neither party achieved a decided advantage ; and when at last Otho's power had been completely broken, and he had been forced to recognise Philip as Emperor, the sword of an assassin, in the pursuit of private revenge, did for him what years of warfare had been unable to accomplish, and, with the death of Philip, he found himself undisputed master of the Empire (A.D. 1208).

In this struggle the genius of Walter von der Vogel-weide was from the first enlisted on the side of Philip of Suabia. And, though it is unnecessary to assume that, in choosing this side, the poet's motives were absolutely disinterested, his political songs belonging to this period have so true a ring, are filled with so unfeigned an admira-tion of and affection for the young Emperor, and so bitter a scorn of those who subordinated the interests of the Empire to their own petty and personal ambitions, that it is impossible not to see in them the expression of a genuine patriotism. For, indeed, the triumph of the house of Hohenstaufen meant the establishment of a united and powerful German state, and the curbing of those disruptive forces which were destined in time to split up the Empire into numberless petty princedoms.

To the early period of the civil war, when the opposing factions were as yet evenly matched, belong the oldest of Walter's political rhymes. In the first he pictures the miserable condition to which the country had been reduced by the civil dissension ; in a second, after illustrating from the analogy of Nature the necessity for a strong Govern-ment, he calls on Germany to set the crown on Philip's head, and curb the ruinous ambition of the petty princes :

These threadbare Kinglets press thee sore :
Crown Philip with the Kaiser's crown,
        and bid them vex thy peace no more !

In a third, perhaps written somewhat later, in 1201, when Innocent III. had pronounced sentence of excommunication on Philip of Suabia, he attacks the clergy and the See of Rome with bitter violence, ascribing to their un-Christian ambition the evils by which, in Germany, Church and State—soul and body—had been made desolate.

For Innocent, whose support had been eagerly sought by both sides, had, after long deliberation and a careful weighing, from his own point of view, of the merits of the rival candidates, finally decided to espouse the cause of Otho. And the casting of the whole weight of the papal influence into the scale on behalf of the weaker and less desirable claimant was but the continuation of the traditional policy of the Curia, which had been accustomed to look for the strength of the Papacy in the weakness of the Empire, and to fear, from a strongly established rule beyond the Alps, a renewal of those imperial claims and ambitions in Italy which, under Henry VI., had confined the temporal sway of the Popes within the walls of the city.

With the death of Philip, and the election and coronation of Otho (A.D. 1208), the policy of Innocent would seem to have been crowned with success. But the very completeness of the triumph of the Guelph once more brought into violent antagonism the rival claims of the spiritual and temporal powers. Even if Otho had been of a more conciliatory temperament, a contest between principles so irreconcilable could hardly have been long avoided. As it was, he hastened the crisis by his violent and aggressive policy. No sooner had the electors raised him to the Empire than he proclaimed himself the champion of the most extreme view of the Divine prerogatives of the imperial dignity. The crown which in the days of his weakness he had declared his willingness to wear 'by the grace of the Pope' he now claimed unconditionally, and as a matter of right; the concessions he had made to the Holy See in respect of the patrimony of Saint Peter, he now refused to ratify, and began to revive all the somewhat indefinite claims of the Empire in Middle Italy.[1]

In the face of these unexpected provocations, Innocent behaved with great moderation and dignity. He did not refuse to crown the Emperor, the ceremony taking place on October 4, 1209, not without the usual riots and bloodshed between the Roman populace and the German 'barbarians.'

[1] Raumer, Band iii., p. 9.

For nearly a year from this time the Pope met the increasing violence of the Emperor with all the arts of patient diplomacy; and not till November 12, 1210, when Otho had declared open war upon the Church, and put his threats of invading Apulia into execution, did he use the last and most potent of his weapons, and launch against him the thunderbolt of excommunication.[1]

The rapid success which attended the young Frederick II. in his apparently hopeless attempt to recover from Otho, with the help of the Holy See, the throne of his ancestors, was doubtless accelerated by the Emperor's unpopular rule,[2] his incapacity, and unbridled temper, and consummated by his overthrow, at the hands of Philip Augustus, on the field of Bouvines (1214). But it was none the less a remarkable proof of the influence exercised at that time over men's minds by the papal censures; and makes all the more remarkable the independence of those who, like Walter von der Vogelweide, without losing their reverence for religion or for the Catholic faith, ventured in no mild terms to criticise the action of the head of — Christendom.

For all through the long contest, which was not to end till many years after he had passed away, Walter had been consistently on the side of the Empire. He had supported —

---

[1] Raumer, Band iii., p. 12.   [2] Id., p. 12.

Philip until his untimely death made Otho the only
possible candidate for the throne ; he then supported Otho
and opposed Frederick II., the 'priests' king,' as he was
contemptuously called ; and when the violence and incapacity of Otho had made his rejection not only inevitable,
but desirable in the interests of the Empire, he was one of
the last to leave the side of the fallen Emperor. Finally,
when Frederick had in his turn fallen under the displea-
sure of the Holy See, it is on the side of the Emperor that
Walter is again found.

But, while we may admire the boldness of Walter's
attitude towards the Papacy, and the honesty of purpose
which dictated it, we may well doubt whether the extreme
language which he uses had any real justification. By the
Ghibelline party, indeed, the anti-papal rhymes were hailed
with unbounded delight, and they became a new and
potent weapon against the pretensions of Rome. To most
modern German critics, too, writing from a Protestant
standpoint, they have appealed as the expression of a just
hatred of a baneful foreign influence, and of a righteous
revolt against the ambition of an unscrupulous priesthood ;
and more than one writer of recent years has furbished up
these ancient weapons for use in modern controversies.
Yet, to the impartial reader of history, they can appear
only as the utterances of an eager if sincere partisanship,

possibly even of a party passion which 'had lost all sense of moderation and dignity.'[1]

This is not the place to enter into a discussion of the principles at issue between the mediæval Papacy and the Empire; but, if we judge the controversy on the plane of motive, it is difficult to avoid the conclusion that in grandeur of aim and singleness of purpose the Popes were the superiors of the Cæsars. And, of all mediæval Popes, the greatest, in the magnificence of his schemes, in the clearness of his outlook, and in the strength and nobility of his personal character, was Innocent III., whom Walter von der Vogelweide denounces as a second Judas, and accuses of being in league with the devil!

Yet, in Walter's most bitter denunciations of Rome, it is the Popes, and not the Papacy, that he attacks. He does, indeed, ask indignantly why, if the Pope be, as he says, Saint Peter's successor, he erases Saint Peter's teaching from his books; and, in another poem, he speaks of the Donation of Constantine as the source of all the woes of the Church. But, in spite of all, the Pope to him is still 'the Lord's shepherd,' though he is become a 'wolf among his flock'; he is God's 'treasurer,' though he 'steals from the heavenly store'; he is Christ's vicar, though 'he robs and slays with fire and sword'!

[1] Wilmanns, *W. v. d. Vogelweide*, vol. i., p. 113.

For Walter remains to the last a pious Christian and a devout Catholic ; and though the number of his still extant religious songs is small, those that remain breathe a spirit of deep and sincere piety : nor is there in any of them a trace of a premature Protestantism, or of any of those heresies which, at that time, had gained so strong a hold in the south of Europe.

It was in the crusading spirit that mediæval piety found its most characteristic expression ; and although, at the end of the twelfth century, this was already on the wane, Walter von der Vogelweide's thoughts, like those of many others, turned often in the direction of the Holy Land ; and in his later years he frequently laments the infirmities of age which prevented him from earning 'that eternal crown, which any churl may gain, with sword and shield and spear.' Moreover, one of the charges which, with no apparent justification,[1] he more than once brings against the Pope, is that of diverting the funds, ostensibly collected to further the Crusades, to the prosecution of schemes of ambition nearer home :

> Little of all this money in God's cause is spent :
> To part with a great treasure priests are ill content.

In his enthusiasm for the cause of Christendom against

---

[1] *Cf.* Wilmanns, vol. i., p. 113.

the infidel, indeed, Walter falls foul of even more exalted
personages than the Pope; and, in a poem of amusing
naïveté, after a couple of stanzas in praise of God and of
the Virgin, he proceeds to scold the three archangels by
name, for neglecting to come to the aid of the Christians
with their undoubtedly great resources:

> Since all unseen ye are and voiceless still,
> Tell us, to help the cause what have ye done?
> If I as silently could wreak
> God's vengeance, think not I would speak!
> I'd leave you gentlemen alone!

But of the religious attitude of Walter von der Vogelweide, perhaps the most remarkable feature is that wide
tolerance which he shared with so many of the nobler
minds of his age, and of which the Emperor Frederick II.
set so conspicuous an example.

The latter had not hesitated to incur the censures of
the Church by surrounding himself with Saracen and
Jewish men of letters, whom he employed to translate into
Latin the Arabic version of Aristotle, and other ancient
and contemporary scientific works; he had made, when in
Palestine, an advantageous treaty on equal terms with the
Sultan of Egypt, and is even reported to have admitted
him to one of the Christian orders of chivalry; and if he
did not extend to heretics the protection which he gave to
infidels, this was because to have done so would have been

to undermine those religious principles on which the mediæval polity was based.

If such was the attitude of the Emperor, that of the poets was no less remarkable. At a time when the crusading spirit was only beginning to show signs of decline ; when, in Germany, Conrad of Marburg, the cruel and fanatical tormentor of the saintly Elizabeth of Hungary, was travelling from town to town, putting hundreds to death on flimsy charges of heresy ; and when the joyous civilisation of Provence was stamped out, in the name of religion, by the barbarous hordes of Simon de Montfort, it is strange indeed to find a didactic writer like the Thuringian priest, Werner von Elmendorf, founding his moral teaching not on the Bible or the rules of the Church, but more particularly on the authority of ancient authors : Seneca, Sallust, Cicero, Lucan, Horace, Ovid, Boethius, and even Xenophon ! ' Solomon,' he says, ' refers us to the ant for an example ; but, if I may learn virtue from an insect, how much more can I receive it from a heathen ! ' [1] The same spirit breathes in that noble passage which, in his epic of ' Willehalm,' Wolfram von Eschenbach places in the mouth of a heathen woman :

> If for a woman's word ye care,
> God's handiwork ye then would spare !

[1] *Cf.* Wilm., vol. i., p. 69. Also Scherer, vol. i., p. 214.

For lo ! a heathen was the man
God made when He his work began.

.   .   .   .   .

As heathens all of us were born.
The saved might well in sorrow mourn,
If he his children should condemn
To hell, who had begotten them ;
His mercy will on them descend,
Whose store of mercy hath no end.

.   .   .   .   .

Whate'er the heathen did to you,
To them ye should no evil do ;
Since God himself gave pardon free
To those who nailed Him on the tree.

This same moral of mutual respect and toleration is enforced also by Walter von der Vogelweide in a remarkable little poem, in which he says that, in the worship of the Creator, ' Christians, Jews, and Heathen all agree.'

It is certain that the political and religious poems of Walter von der Vogelweide exercised a deep and widespread influence. By a Guelph partisan[1] he is accused of leading thousands astray ; and at a time when newspapers and political pamphlets were undreamed of, his stirring rhymes, whether recited by himself at some great meeting of the feudal chiefs, or repeated from mouth to mouth among the people, became a force to be reckoned with and respected.

Of Walter's private life little is known with any cer-

[1] Thomasin of Zirclaria. Cf. Wilm., vol i., p. 113.

tainty. Famous as he was, there is only one mention of his name in contemporary records—an entry in the travelling accounts of Bishop Wolfger of Passau : ' Walthero cantori de Vogelweide pro pellicio V solidos longos ' (to Walter the singer of the Vogelweide, 5 shillings for a fur coat !). The good prelate seems to have been very free-handed towards minstrels, jugglers, and ' travelling folk ' generally, but, besides Walter, only two are mentioned by name : a ' joculator ' Flordamor in Bologna, and a ' mimus ' Giliotho in Aquapendente. This juxtaposition of names would alone seem to imply that Walter was regarded by his princely patrons only in the light of a humble retainer. And indeed, though undoubtedly of noble birth, his own surname proves that he belonged to the lowest grade of nobility : that numerous class of petty nobles (Dienst-adel) who, in war-time, served to swell the train of the great feudal chiefs, and in time of peace were content to perform functions almost menial. For ' Vogelweide ' is the gathering-place or feeding-ground of birds (the Latin *aviarium*), and we have to picture to ourselves the home of Walter's boyhood, not as some lordly castle or stately mansion, but as an obscure lodge hidden away in the forest, probably the falconry attached to the manor of some great lord.

Beyond these vague deductions nothing is known either of Walter's birthplace or parentage. Of late years, indeed, some attempts have been made to establish the site of his home ; and the 'Vogelweiderhof,' near Bozen in the Tyrol, is pointed out as the place of his birth. But, as a matter of fact, the first certain information we have about his early days is that which he himself tells us :

In Austria I learned to say and sing.

If, as most authorities agree, he was born in the Tyrol, the young aspirant to the honours of minstrelsy would naturally have found his way first to the court of Vienna. For here the Duke Leopold V. had established a brilliant centre of art and culture ; and his court was illustrated by the presence of the great Minnesinger Reinmar, to whose memory Walter later on dedicated two of his most beautiful poems. At Vienna Walter remained for some nine years, profiting by the example, if not the actual tuition, of Reinmar,[1] until the death of Duke Leopold's son and successor, Frederick I., broke up the circle of poets who had lived by his patronage (A.D. 1198).

To this period of his life at Vienna, while the poet was still young and full of hope, belong the best and most charming of his love lyrics, and it is to these early days that, in after years, when age, poverty, and the miseries of

---

[1] Wilmanns says that Walter was the rival, not the pupil, of Reinmar, and suggests, from somewhat insufficient internal evidence, that he was educated in a monastic school.

the times had all but broken his spirit, he looks back as to a golden age.

For with the death of this, the first and most generous of his patrons, seems to have begun for him a life of struggle, and at times almost of destitution :

> When it to Frederick of Austria did betide
> That he his soul did save, the while his body died,
> My crane-like steps were hid with him in earth.
> Then crawled I like a peacock whereso'er I went ;
> Down to my very knees my head I humbly bent.

From this time onward he appears to have travelled from court to court, depending for a living on the uncertain patronage of various princes ; and this during a period when the civil wars can have left them little time for art and artists. And always his heart yearns for the old life at Vienna, and he addresses eloquent appeals to Duke Leopold VI. to restore him to his favour :

> Closed to me now is fortune's gate,
> Lo ! orphanlike outside I wait,
> And all my knocking helps me not a whit.

Whether these prayers had any effect is not clear. But, even if Walter returned to Vienna, it was not for long, and he was soon cast adrift again to seek for other patrons.

In this 'juggler's life,' as he himself calls it, Walter

experienced all the moods of the fickle goddess. At one time he is happy in the favour of some great prince : of Philip of Suabia, of the Emperor Otho (who appears, however, to have been more lavish of promises than gifts), of the Margrave of Meissen, or the Landgrave of Thuringia. At other times we find him complaining good-humouredly of the unkindness of Fortune, who showers favours on others, but always turns her back on him ; or, in a more depressed vein, addressing earnest appeals for help to princes who, too often, alas ! ' will not hear,' and complaining that though ' rich in art,' he is yet ' plunged in poverty.' For Walter was, like the rest of his class, not ashamed to beg ; and though he never stooped to solicit help by degrading flattery, those who spared their money at his expense were apt to feel the lash of his tongue.

Yet, in spite of prayers and scoldings, and of his vast popularity, he lived the greater part of his life a poor man, dependent for house and home on the generosity of those whom he entertained with his art ; until at last the Emperor Frederick II. rewarded his services by the grant of a small fief in the neighbourhood of Würzburg, and thus preserved his declining years from want. Whether or not the Emperor bestowed upon him a still more signal proof of his favour, in entrusting to him the tuition of his young son, King Henry VII., would seem to be uncertain, the evidence for this somewhat surprising fact resting almost entirely on a single poem,[1] and that one which, though it undoubtedly seems to favour this view, is capable of another interpretation. It seems, indeed, highly improbable that the Emperor should have given so great a charge as the education of his eldest son to a wandering minstrel, however celebrated. But, even if this was the case, the perverse and intractable disposition of the young prince would seem to have soon compelled him to resign his charge, though he continued to enjoy the favour of the Emperor till his death. He died about the year 1230, and was buried at Würzburg, where, though his monument has been defaced, his remains rest at the present day.

To the sterling and lovable qualities of Walter von der Vogelweide's character there are two trustworthy sources of evidence—his own poems and the witness of his contemporaries. In the former we have revealed to us a man who, in an age of storm and stress, full of dangerous chances, and pregnant with doubtful issues, was consistent in his allegiance to the cause which from the first he had recognised as that of his country; a man of deep religious feeling, yet of wide sympathies, scornful of mere superstition, and uncompromising in his opposition to the ambition of the priesthood; a poor man, who yet maintained his

[1] *See* page 121.

independence of speech; and one whose wit, in an age not over-refined, never descended to coarseness. And, amid all his trials and disappointments, one supreme satisfaction at least was not denied him: that of knowing himself to be appreciated at his full worth by his contemporaries. To his fellow-singers, indeed, he was the prince of minstrels: the 'Master'—*unsers sanges meister*—as they loved to call him; and, when he died, there were many found to celebrate his memory in song. Of these appreciations, the simplest and, by reason perhaps of its very simplicity, the most eloquent is that of Hugo von Trimberg:

> Her Walther von der Vogelweide
> Wer des vergaes der taet mir leide!
>
> (Sir Walter von der Vogelweide
> I pity them that him forget!)

TO

WALTER VON DER VOGELWEIDE

MASTER, whose voice, uprising clear and strong
Across the strife of centuries, we hear ;
To whom, amid thy peers without a peer,
Through all the length of ages shall belong
A place among the deathless kings of song,
By right divine of thine own excellence ;
Whose art was as a sword for the defence
Of goodness, and the chastisement of wrong —
Thy song still lives, though thou art gone to dust ;
And still the sharp lash of thy scornful tongue
May scourge the feeble rhymesters of our day,
Who sing a love half sicklied into lust,
And, for the springs of beauty, grope among
The iridescent foulness of decay.

W. A. P.

1896.

D

IN the following poems certain peculiarities, which will strike a modern, and especially an English reader, may perhaps stand in need of a word of explanation. First, in regard to the somewhat singular way in which abstract ideas are personified—a favourite device of the mediæval German poets. The virtues, such as Moderation, Steadfastness, Constancy, and the like, are represented as women. As a woman, too, the World is personified, beautiful in face, but unspeakably dreadful and revolting of aspect when she turns her back. Fortune is already known to us as a lady of fickle temperament ; but Love, in the guise of a goddess, armed, like Diana, with a bow and arrows, is less familiar. The month of May, on the other hand, which we have been accustomed to picture to ourselves as a maiden, robed in gossamer and garlanded with flowers, we are surprised to find represented as a man, with something even martial in his aspect, coming, as he does, to his high festival as to a tournament, with all his forces (*mit aller siner krefte*), and wearing his floral splendours somewhat after the manner of heraldic blazonry.

With regard to the form of the poems, also, a few words may not be out of place, as in the translations I have endeavoured to keep that of the originals. Mediæval German lyrics are broadly divided into two classes : the song proper (*das liet*), and the short poem intended more especially for recitation (*der spruch*). To 'sing and say' (*singen ünde sagen*) was the technical expression for these two forms. The first was a song in the actual sense of the word, for to its completeness belonged not only the metrical form (*don*) and the subject-matter (*wort*), but also the melody (*wîse*), and every poet was at the same time composer and performer. The songs were generally accompanied by a stringed instrument—a fiddle or small harp.

The most important characteristic of the song (*liet*), in its latest and completest development, was, however, the threefold division of the strophe : the first two parts to introduce and develop the verse, the third to combine and complete the other two. The Meistersingers, who borrowed this form from the Minnesingers (it is enlarged upon in the first Act of Wagner's Opera), to describe the constituent elements, had recourse to the terminology of architecture.

The first two parts were called ' Stollen,' *i.e.* door-posts, to which the 'Abgesang,' the concluding or third part, stood in the relation of the lintel, which at once supports and is supported by them. This tripartite division, much modified, may be traced in the sonnet, where at any rate the principle of cohesion is still the same.

Upon this uniform ground-plan a metrical system of endless variety was erected ; for to borrow, except for purposes of parody, the metre or melody of others, or even to repeat the same metre often, was considered a sign of want of skill, and the ingenuity of the poets was taxed to the uttermost to discover new and complicated forms. This will account for, and I hope excuse, some of the rather cruel metres to be found among the following poems.

In some of the longer poems a certain want of cohesion is apparent, which may perhaps be accounted for by the importance, greater then than now, of the individual strophe in relation to the whole ; for the songs of the earlier Minnesingers were never of more than one verse, and when several came to be combined in a single poem it was spoken of, not as a unit, but in the plural (*diu liet*).

In some of Walter's earlier songs the threefold division

is not as yet developed, and they retain some of the character of the older epic forms.

The 'Spruch' consists always of but one verse, and the tripartite division is by no means always present. It is the form in which the political, didactic, and occasional poems are for the most part cast, the 'liet' being the form used for the love songs.

POEMS

THE POWER OF LOVE

WHAT gave thee thy strange empire, Love,
　　　That thou art so exceeding strong?
　　　Both young and old thy puissance prove,
　　And no one may resist thee long!
Praise God then, since I must be bound
With thy firm bonds, that I betimes have found
Where service best may offered be!
That will I ne'er renounce!　Be gracious, Queen!
　Let me henceforward give my life to thee!

LOVE IS TWO HEARTS' HAPPINESS

CAN any tell me what love is ?
In part I know, but fain would know yet more.
If anyone can answer this,
Let him now tell me why it hurts so sore.
Love is love if it be kind,
But if it hurt, it is not well called love ;
Yet what its real name I cannot find.

If it so chance I rightly guess
What love may be, I beg you to approve.
Love is two hearts' happiness !
If both have part therein, then is it love.
But, if both have not a share,
One heart alone cannot contain it all ;
Woe's me ! Would'st thou but help me, lady fair !

LOVE IS TWO HEARTS' HAPPINESS

Lady, alone I am o'erweighted :
If thou wilt aid me, do not long delay !
But if for all my love I am but hated,
Tell me at once, and I will yield the day,
And shall once again be free !
But this then shalt thou learn, that none more skilled
   Than I to sing a lay in praise of thee !

Can my fair give sour for sweet ?
Or thinks she I will yield her love for hate ?
Shall I but worship at her feet
That she may spurn me for my lowly state ?
I were but a purblind wight—
Woe's me !　What said I, eyeless, earless fool ?
   Whom love hath blinded, how should he have sight ?

LET him who thinks that love is sin,
    Ere he speak out, bethink him well ;
    For thousand virtues dwell therein
And happiness immutable,
Which all who strive to win it rightly may attain.
Whenever anyone misdoes, love suffers pain.
False love by this I do not mean,
Unlove that would be better hight—
That will I ever hate outright.

√

SPRINGTIME AND WOMAN

WHEN flowers through the grass begin to spring,
    As though to greet with smiles the sun's
        bright rays,
On some May morning, and, in joyous measure,
    Small song-birds make the dewy forest ring.
With a shrill chorus of sweet roundelays,
Hath life in all its store a purer pleasure?
    'Tis half a paradise on earth!
    Yet, ask me what I hold of equal worth,
And I will tell what better still
Ofttimes before hath pleased mine eyes,
    And, while I see it, ever will!

    When a noble maiden, fair and pure,
With raiment rich, and tresses deftly braided,
Mingles, for pleasure's sake, in company,
    High-bred, with eyes that, laughingly demure,
Glance round at times, and make all else seem faded,
As, when the sun shines, all the stars must die:
    Let May bud forth in all his splendour,
    What sight so sweet can he engender
As with this picture to compare?
Unheeded leave we buds and blooms,
    And gaze upon the lovely fair!

Then come, if ye the rivals would compare,
To May's high festival let us go forth,
Who to the strife is come with all his forces!
   Look on him well, and on a maiden fair,
And tell me which possess the greater worth
Or whether, of the twain, my choice the worse is.
   Were I, alas! constrained to choose
   Which of these two I would be fain to lose,
My choice, i' faith, would not be slow!
Sir May, ye should be March again,
   Ere I my mistress would forego.

MAY SONG

LOOK how rich a store of treasures
    May with him hath brought!
  Wise and simple, mark the pleasures
  He for us hath wrought.
Puissant is his reign!
What his magic no one knoweth:
Only that, where'er he goeth,
All grow young again.

Sweet delights for us he's bringing:
    Let us joyful be!
Join in dancing, laughing, singing,
    Yet with courtesy!
Ah, who would be sad?
Birds their sweetest lays are trilling,
All the wood with gladness filling;
Let us too be glad!

Welcome, May! In all thou wakest
    Sweetest rivalry!
Lo, the meadows fair thou deckest,
    Fairer than the tree.
Brighter are they dressed:
'Thou art under, I am over!'
Thus the daisies and the clover
In the fields contest.

15

Rosy mouth, ah, why so scornful?
   Let thy laughter be!
Shame, that that which makes me mournful
   Should give joy to thee!
Lady, is this right?
Wasted were these hours of anguish,
If thou bid me ever languish
Thus, in love's despite!

Lady, thou my joy art stealing
   With thy loveliness.
Thou alone canst grant me healing,
   Yet art merciless!
Why so hard of heart?
Store of joy could'st thou have lent me,
Yet with coldness dost torment me,
Cruel that thou art!

Save me, lady, from my sorrow;
   Fill my days with bliss;
Joys from thee I needs must borrow
   Which through thee I miss!
Look around, and see:
All the world is full of pleasure:
Ah, that but a tiny measure
Might be left for me!

A KISS FROM ROSY LIPS

OH! would my dearest mistress but consent
      To go with me and gather roses ever,
    I'd fill the hours with such sweet argument
That not all time our bond of love should sever ;
If from her rosy lips that so enchant me
One kiss she'd grant me,
A bliss more perfect I would ask for never.

PRAISE OF SUMMER

WHAT though the heath with thousand colours glow,
    Yet to the woodland must I needs confess
    That richer store of pleasures it can show,
And fairer still the meadows' loveliness.
Then Summer, hail, with thy sweet industry!
Summer, that I may never praise thee less,
My comfort! Help me now in my distress!
This is my plaint; I'll tell it thee: She whom
    I love, she loves not me!

Forget her goodness I nor will nor may;
    And, while I sing, I'll find new words to tell
My love for her who steals my thoughts away,
    And praise the virtues that I know so well!
Of my intent let this the earnest be:
The eyes are blest that look upon my sweet,
And blest the ears that hear, when they repeat
Her virtues manifold! May joy be hers!
    Alas for me!

THE ORACLE

I SAT in doubt and direst woe,
    Pondering sadly, and bethought me
  Her service I must needs forego,
  When back once more a comfort brought me.
Alas for comfort it sufficeth not!
  'Tis but a drop of comfort after all;
  Ye'll laugh to hear of it, it is so small;
Yet none find solace in they know not what!   *all*

A straw it is that gladdens me:
  It says that I shall win my wooing;
The blade I measured carefully,
  As I had seen the children doing.
Will she be kind?   Now hark to what it saith:
  'She will, she won't, she will, she won't, she will!'
  Oft as I ask, that is the answer still.
That comforts me—although it need some faith!

Although I love her from my heart,
  Yet little reck I if unto her
Come those who fain would ape my art,
  Nor am I jealous tho' they woo her:
For never, knowing her, would I believe
  That anyone could lightly turn her mind;
  Though to these boasters she be far too kind,
'Tis well they know the cause, if she deceive.

J

MUTUAL LOVE

A RT thou indifferent?
  I do not know: only that I love thee!
  Yet am I ill content
That, when we meet, thou wilt not look at me.
  Torment me thus no more!
  Such wooing would weigh sore
Upon me, had I long to bear it!
My burden now is great: Wilt thou not share it?

  Or is it modesty
That makes thee look so seldom in my eyes?
  If for my sake it be,
Be sure I would not have it otherwise!
  So then, avoid my face!
  (Thus far I give thee grace)
But then, for greeting, when we meet,
  At very least look downward at my feet!

MUTUAL LOVE

Mid all the maids I see
Whose grace and beauty I may justly praise,
  I yield the crown to thee,
Who art my lady, and shalt be always!
  Some among them I find
  Rich and of lofty mind,
As well beseems their noble blood :
More noble they may be, but thou art good !

  Mistress mine, now say,
Whether thou have not any love for me !
  My love is thrown away,
If it be doomed ever alone to be,
  Love dies if it be lonely
  And lives in common only :
So far in common that it stay
Fixed in two hearts, and never further stray.

GOD be with thee, dearest maid,
And fill thy days with happiness !
Could a fairer pray'r be said,
'Twould better all my heart express.
What could I now tell thee more
Than that none loves thee as I love ? Alas, 'tis
this that wounds me sore !

They blame me that I tune my song
In praise of one not nobly born :
Then, since they judge so strangely wrong
Of what love is, their blame I scorn !
To such as these love never came :
For beauty and for wealth is all their care : Alas,
such love is shame !

22

BEAUTY AND CHARM

Baseness with beauty often goes :
  Too much let none for beauty care.
Charm more upon the heart bestows :
  For charm hath virtue far more rare.
Charm lends a woman loveliness :
But beauty cannot give her charm, so then is
    beauty's power less.

I ne'er was moved, nor am I now,
  By all their sneers, nor shall they move me ;
Lovely, and rich enough, art thou !
  They lose their pains who would reprove me.
I love thee, dear, though they may scold,
And deem thy ring of glass more precious than
    a coronet of gold !

If truth and constancy are thine,
  Then am I thine, nor fear distress
Will fall upon this heart of mine,
  Wounded by thee in wantonness.
But ah ! if thou have not these twain,
Then mayest thou never more be mine : Alas,
    and I had loved in vain !

J

A DREAM OF LOVE

'LADY, accept this wreath!'
　　Thus spake I to a maiden debonair,
　　'And thy sweet face beneath
　'The lovely flow'rs will make the dance more fair!
If precious stones were mine,
They should adorn thy head;
This is not idly said:
All that I have, and all I am, is thine!

'So sweet and fair art thou,
　My fairest chaplet gladly I bestow
To place upon thy brow.
　Rich store of flowers white and red I know
In fields afar; in the May weather,
Now that the buds are springing,
And the wild birds singing,
Let us go forth to gather them together!'

24

She took my offering,
 Like a young child to whom a gift is made,
Her fair cheeks colouring
 Like a red rose beside a lily laid ;
Yet though, as if ashamed, her eyelids fell,
She made a courtesy—
That was her gift to me :
If she gave more, be sure I will not tell.

To me it seemed that never
 Could any joy the joy of that surpass ;
From the branches ever
 Blossoms fell thick around us on the grass ;
Lo! and I laughed for very gladness' sake,
Such, in my dream, of pleasure
Store had I beyond measure.
Then dawned the day, and I must needs awake.

From her then, in this wise,
 It comes that, when I meet a maid this year
I gaze into her eyes :
 Can this be she ? Could I but find her here
Among the dancers, all my pain were dead !
Lady, be so good
And lift me up your hood :
Could I but find my chaplet on her head !

LOVE'S JOY

WHAT dreams and hopes have I now lost
    Which on this happy season I had set !
    The cares that came with winter's frost
  In summer I had trusted to forget ;
Thus dreams of better days I cherished,
And, though a thousand joys had perished,
Hope of delight I would not quit.
Alas ! and yet it failed me ever,
For joy so constant found I never
But tired of me, ere I of it.

Since then no joy will stay with me,
  There were small cause to praise my happiness ;
If one so fortunate there be
  That he his lady's favour doth possess,
If he be joyous too, and glad
(Alas, and I the while so sad !),

Let him not lightly mock at me
Because his lady-love is kind :
I too would have a cheerful mind,
Were but my mistress kind to me.

O happy man ! O happy maid !
    Whose hearts united nought may sever !
I pray that honour may be paid
    And praise to such as these for ever !
Joyous and sweet may all their moments be !
Aye, and a happy man is he
Who, looking on them, doth aspire
To imitate their faithfulness :
Him may a noble woman bless,
And grant him all his heart's desire !

Some think that they are living well
    Who in good women's service do not live ;
Ah, luckless fools ! they cannot tell
    What joy and lofty honour love may give.
Light-minded people, it is plain,
Will ever of light things be fain :
Whoso would joy and honour win,
Let him a woman's favour earn ;
If freely she his love return,
Honour and joy he'll find therein !

Lord! what a strange conceit hath he
   Who, without service, not in vain hath loved!
Woman or man, whiche'er it be
   That thus can love, and watch the while unmoved
Good service rendered, should be held but low.
A noble woman acts not so:
She marks a man's high character,
And learns by this the bad to shun;
A foolish has such ways, that none
But fools would care to follow her.

LOVE, THE CONQUEROR

ALAS for me, unhappy wight !
     Why do I hearts with gladness fill
     Which never may my pains requite ?
Ah ! why do friends behave so ill ?
Friends ! Idle talk of friends indeed :
Had I a friend, he'd to my grief give heed.
Friendless am I and counsel-less ;
So treat me as thou wilt, most lovely Love,
    Since no one pities my distress !

Most lovely Love, 'tis thou alone
    My senses all hast stol'n away,
Who in my heart hast set thy throne
    To rule with undivided sway !
Sans senses what will come of me ?
Since thou now dwellest where their place should be :
Thou sent'st them forth thou knowest whither,
Alas, unaided they will woo in vain !
    Queen Love, would'st thou but follow thither !

Ah, Mistress Love, be kind! If thou
   This errand wilt but do for me,
Ever to thy commands I'll bow.
   Then, prithee, treat me graciously!
Full is her heart of happiness,
And every grace of virtue doth possess :
If there thou canst set up thy throne,
Then let me in, that both of us may woo her—
   I should but fail, were I to plead alone!

Love, have but mercy, and forbear!
   Why wilt thou only torture me ?
I am thy slave, now conquer her :
   Try if she will not yield to thee.
Now shall I tell how strong thou art.
Thou darest not say thou canst not force her heart :
Ne'er lock had wards so manifold
As to resist thee long, thou Queen of thieves!
   Open! against thee she's too bold!

VIRTUE AND CHARM

SUMMER returned, the year renewed,
  A trusty hope, a dream divine,
  These set me in so gay a mood :
Surely some joy will yet be mine !
  I know of something far more fair
Than all the wild-birds' minstrelsies :
A woman's beauty everywhere
Will to no rival yield the prize.
  Then ah, what store of happiness
In my sweet mistress I possess !
For fairer than the fair is she,
If charm the crown of beauty be.

Full well I know 'tis charm that gives
Her beauty to a woman fair ;
Yet when a woman nobly lives,
For her it is we most should care.
  Better than gold and pearls combined
Will charm with beauty ever fit :
Add to these twain a noble mind,
And tell me, what could better it ?
  These raise a man in worthiness.
He also who love's sweet distress
Knows, for their sakes, to bear aright,
May sing indeed of heart's delight.

The glance which a sweet woman throws
On him she loves makes glad the heart ;
Ah then, what would you say of those
Who in her favour have more part ?
　These still are rich in happiness,
When all that brief delight is spent.
What greater joy than to possess
A woman's heart, being confident
　That it is faithful, pure, and wise ?
If one be blessed with such a prize,
Should he to others sing his bliss,
Be sure he is no fool in this !

Ah, luckless wight who does not care
To sue for a good woman's love !
Though she should never grant his pray'r,
'Twould none the less a blessing prove.
　Let him but, for one woman's sake,
So act that he shall please the rest,
Him will another happy make,
Though this one grant not his request.
　Let noble men consider this,
For honour lies therein and bliss.
He who good woman's love doth heed
Will blush to do an evil deed.

THE ENCHANTRESS

I MUST ever marvel what a maid
    Can have approved in me
      That her enchantment on me she hath laid.
  What can the reason be ?
Surely she too hath eyes :
    How comes it that she sees so badly then ?
    Troth, I am not the handsomest of men,
That nobody denies.

If she of me false witness have believed,
    Let her now use her own.
As to my looks she hath been sore deceived,
    If she seek these alone.
Let her but see my face !
    Trust me, she'll find it is exceeding plain ;
    If she believe not, she but dreams in vain
That beauty there has place.

Near her there are a thousand more or less
    Far handsomer than I.
Save that I boast a little cleverness,
    The world would pass me by
True, I am somewhat clever,
    But in such wise as one may often see ;
    My gifts are such as are not like to be
Other than common ever.

If wit in place of beauty she will take,
    I would indeed commend her,
For then, whate'er she venture for my sake
    But a new grace would lend her.
To her then will I bow,
    And all her wishes study to fulfil ;
    What need to use so much enchantment still ?
I am her bondman now !

Now hear the secret of her magic art,
    Which lends her so great power ;
A fair faced maid she is, and pure of heart,
    With joy undimmed for dower !
I say not (that may God forfend !)
    That other magic art she doth possess,
    Save the enchantment of her loveliness
Which pain or joy can send.

IF I were sad, 'twould turn me back to gladness
  To speak in noble women's praise,
For this I ever found, to banish sadness,
  The sweetest and the best of ways.
Happy am I that, when I tell
  Their praises, it should give them joy,
And profit me as well!

Ah! if but one fair lady would allow me,
  I'd make an end of sorrowing.
Alas! but niggard favour will she show me
  For all the service that I bring.
My praise she loves, and deems it good:
  But me she evermore forgets,
And her own gratitude.

Strange women oft with fairest thanks receive me:
  I pray that they may happy be!
Beside the guerdon that my fair should give me
  Such thanks have little worth for me.
But let her use me as she will!
  Good-will I have: my works I blame
If these be wanting still.

LOVE'S LABOUR LOST

MY mistress is a most ungracious maid
       To use me ever so exceeding ill!
    When first my homage at her feet I paid,
  Young were my years, and high my courage still.
Alas! how joyous then was I.
How all is turned to pain!
For what has been my gain?
Naught save the grief for woe of which I sigh.

Alas, for all my tale of happy days!
    How many for her sake I spent in vain!
Good cause my heart will have to grieve always
    If all my pleasure thus be lost in pain.
For what I bear of grief and woe,
I make but little moan ;
It is my time alone
Which, if it be all wasted, grieves me so.

Never yet saw I face so wondrous fair ;
　　Into her heart, alas, I could not see !
And so the while I was deceived in her,
　　And thus my faith it was that ruined me.
If all the stars in heaven,
The moon, too, and the sun,
I by my wits had won,
To her, upon my soul, they had been given !

Never yet saw I ways so passing strange
　　That she should quarrel with her truest friend ;
Yet with her foes she shrinks not to exchange
　　Whispers : Which can have but an ill end !
Well know I what this end will be :
Friend as well as foes
She is like to lose,
If she in such wise use both them and me.

'Tis not on me that she must lay the blame,
　　If forth in quest to foreign lands I go,
Seeking for maids who have a kindly fame
　　For tenderness (and many such I know !),
And whose faces too are fair.
Yet not one of all,
Be she great or small,
Is there whose nay could drive me to despair.

ABSENT YET PRESENT

MY lady sometimes comes to me;
   So sweet is she, I know it must be so,
      Since I from her can never absent be.
If it be true that love to love must go,
   Then will she oftentimes in thought
Play truant, as I do as well.
My body's here, my soul with her doth dwell;
And thence may nevermore be brought.
I pray that it may watch my sweet for me,
And not forget myself the while!
Of what avail to shut my eyes?
Since through my heart they can as clearly see!

LOVE'S PREROGATIVE

BLAME me not if, when I meet you,
Lady, I so coldly greet you.
Love with love may angry be,
So it be but lovingly.
Softly chide, and quick forgive,
Sorrow and grow glad again,
That is Love's prerogative!

FORTUNE'S UNKINDNESS

DAME FORTUNE scatters gifts about me,
  But always turns on me her back !
  And thus it comes she needs must scout me,
 And counsel in this strait I lack !
For show her face she never will :
If I run round, I am behind her still ;
 She will not deign to look at me.
I would her eyes were in her back !
 Then, willy nilly, she would have to see !

IS it an evil or is it good
   That I my sorrow can disguise?
      For joyous often seems my mood
While many another weeps and sighs
   Who never knew one half my miseries.
I bear myself as though I had
Rich store of joy to make me glad.
I pray that God my future may dispense,
That happiness I yet may have without pretence!

   How comes it that I comfort bring
To many a lover in despair,
   Yet know for my own suffering
No cure, save to disguise my care?
   I love a maiden, sweet she is and fair:
To my first words she will attend,
But never hears me to the end.
One thing alone saves me from desperation—
She smiles a little, when she turns the conversation.

   If she well guard her heart within
(Without she is surpassing fair),
   And harbour no unkindly sin,
Never yet maid had charm so rare:

No other woman can with her compare,
If but her outward loveliness
The beauty of her soul express ;
Could I but serve her in some poor degree,
So sweet a mistress surely would not thankless be !

What though my joy be doubtful still
Which yet my sweet to certainty
  Could turn at once, had she the will,
I fret not at my misery.
  One thing she asks that should unquestioned be—
How long my love for her will live ;
There is no other maid can give
The hope of joy that she in me doth stir :
Ah, would she but reward me for my faith in her !

Many into their true love's ear
Can speak with greater eloquence ;
  But I, when she is sitting near,
Am like a child for diffidence,
  And blindness falls upon my every sense.
Others for this would laugh at me :
So sweet and good a maid is she,
She wants no words, if she can find good will.
And that I have, as I may hope for comfort still !

LOVE'S CREED

MANY there are that mock my pain,
    And ever say that 'tis not truly from the
      heart I sing;
  These but spend their breath in vain,
Since they can never yet have known love's joy and
    suffering;
  And so it is they judge me wrong:
Whoever knows
All that from true love flows,
Would not misunderstand my song.

  Love is but a common word,
Yet most uncommon in its works, such pow'r doth it
    possess!
  Love is of every joy the hoard;
The heart that knows not love can know no real happi-
    ness.
  Since then this is my belief,
Mistress Love,
Show me thou dost approve!
Let not my joy be turned to grief!

My hope is, that the maid I love
Truly, and in all honesty, may yield me love again.
   If this hope unfounded prove,
But little joy 'twill bring me, and my dream will all be
      vain.
   God forbid !   She is so sweet,
When she doth know
That I do love her so,
She'll make my happiness complete.

   If my true heart she could but see,
Love and the happiness I ask she'd grant me readily.
   But alas ! how may that be,
Since false love too woos nowadays with such sweet
      minstrelsy
   That a maid can never know
Who speaks truth ?
This wrong hath been, in sooth,
Ofttimes the cause of lovers' woe.

   Whoever first a maid deceived
Wrought a great and grievous wrong to men as well as
      maids ;
   Since vows no more can be believed,
Who may marvel much if love itself grows faint and fades ?

LOVE'S CREED

Sweet, God spare you this distress!
And grant me yet
The balance of love's debt
As guerdon for my faithfulness!

UNEQUAL JUSTICE

I SANG her praise so constantly
    That many in the world now hold her high.
If this is why she punish me,
    Then but a fool for all my pains was I
Thus to have extolled her name,
And with praise adorned
One who my gifts hath scorned.
Mistress Love, 'tis thee for this I blame!

This too my plaint is, Mistress Love:
    Help me to right, and judge me righteously!
Since it was I that ever strove
    For thy good name 'gainst men's inconstancy.
I am wounded in the strife!
Thou hast piercèd me,
While unscathed is she:
She is whole, the while I lose my life!

Mistress, reward the toil I spent !
   Arrows are in thy quiver left, I know :
Into her heart let one be sent,
   That she and I may feel the selfsame woe !
Oh ! noble Queen, cause her, I pray,
To feel what I now feel,
Or else my own hurt heal !
Must I be forced alone to waste away ?

Mistress Love, thou holdest me !
   At those take aim that still thy pow'r defy !
Help me to the victory !
   Nay, lady, haste, lest she thine arrows fly !
I will say how that would end :
If she escape thy dart
Thou and I must part ;
And who to thee again would suppliant bend ?

LOVE'S HAPPINESS

NEVER before had I such hope of bliss!
       And hence it comes that I perforce must sing.
   · Hail to the maid who shall requite me this!
   To her pure worth it is my song I bring.
She who my heart in bonds doth hold
All my sorrows now may end me,
And may send me
Pleasures manifold.

If God grant that I my wooing win,
   Lo, then would I rejoice for evermore!
With happiness she fills my heart within
   As never woman else could do before!
Hitherto I did not know
That Love e'er binds and looses
Where he chooses,
Till she taught me so.

LOVE'S HAPPINESS

Sweet Love, since then the maid but followed thee
   In binding thus my heart with tender chains,
Her gentle favours bid her yield to me,
   That I may have surcease of all my pains!
Through the bright glance of her eyes
She so winsomely received me,
All that grieved me
Vanished in a trice!

Glad am I that I serve so good a maid,
   In hope that love's reward may yet be mine:
And oft this comfort all my sorrow stayed,
   And caused my heart's unhappiness to pine.
If indeed she end my woe,
Then shall I in truth discover
Never lover
Such delight did know.

Love, from thy favour what delights arise!
   What pleasures perish through thy cruelty,
When pain thou biddest laugh from sparkling eyes,
   In wanton proof of thy strange mastery!
Thou canst suddenly make sad
Hearts with joy abounding,
Since thy wounding
Mournful makes and glad.

LOVE'S MAGIC

LORD GOD, from care and misery defend me,
That I may live right happily!
If anyone his happiness would lend me,
And asks for good security,
That would I quickly find I well know where :
For store of pleasures left I there,
Of which, with subtle art,
I hope to gain a part.

'Tis in a maid lies all my wealth of pleasure.
Her heart of virtues hath such store,
Of beauties is her form so rich a treasure,
That I could serve her evermore.
A smile at least I may aspire to gain !
That surely I'll not ask in vain :
She is too sweet to use me
So ill as to refuse me.

Sometimes, when leave to sit with her she grants me,
And I my passion would confess,
It is as though with magic she enchants me,
And strikes my wits with giddiness.
Though now I wondrous eloquent can be,
If she but once do look at me,
My eloquence is gone.
As well to sit alone !

COMFORT IN SORROW

WILL no one e'er again be glad,
　　And must we live for ever sunk in care?
　　Alas! why are the young so sad,
Who ought for very joy to float in air?
　I know not whom I else should blame for this,
Unless I chide the rich, and young in years;
They are free from cares:
Sorrow then suits them ill, and joy were less amiss.

　How strangely Fortune cuts a dress!
She fits high spirits to my poverty,
　Yet clothes in such unhappiness
A wealthy man: What use for wealth has he?
　Me hath Dame Fortune surely clean forgot,
Since she his riches to my merry mind
Sewed not—and she so kind!
Yet better with his gloom had matched my threadbare lot!

COMFORT IN SORROW

Let him on whom a trouble weighs
Think of a noble maid—and he'll be free !
    Or dream of sunny summer days—
The thought that ever most did comfort me.
    For winter's days of gloom fill me with dread,
And solace then I from the meadows borrow,
Which, blushing for their sorrow,
What time they see the woods grow green, turn rosy red.

    Lady, whene'er I think of thee,
How full thy pure soul is of every grace.
    Ah, Sweet, forbear ! Thou woundest me
Deep in my inmost heart, where love has place.
    Not dear, nor dearer will sufficient prove
To name thee, who art dearest of them all !
Henceforth, whate'er befall,
In all the world 'tis thee alone I love.

M Y heart is now so glad and free
There seems no task too hard for my
emprise.
Perchance it may be given to me
To win my lady's favour in some wise :
Lo, and all my senses rise
Far higher than the sunshine ! Queen, listen to my sighs !

Never have I of her had sight
So often, but that when I see my fair,
My eyes for joy of her grow bright.
For winter's cold then little did I care :
To others it seemed hard to bear,
For me it seemed the midst of May the while that she was
there.

LOVE'S JOY

In honour of my lady-love
  Have I now sung this sweet and joyous strain.
Ah, if she do but grateful prove,
  Through her what wealth of pleasure shall I gain !
True, she may cause me pain :
What then, if she should wound me ? Can she not make
    me whole again ?

None shall now on me prevail
  From her my thoughts to sever in despair.
For, if my hope in her should fail,
  How could I find such loveliness elsewhere,
Or guilelessness so rare ?
Nobler than Helen or than Dian is she, and more fair !

NEVER yet saw I days so swiftly flying
    As mine now do ; I watch them as they go.
    I would I knew to whom they can be hieing !
Ever I marvel why they hasten so.
It may be that they will but come
    To those who'll use them not so well as I !
    Well ! let them shine, though they know not on whom !

WINTER

WINTER has wrought us harm everywhere :
Forest and field are dreary and bare
Where the sweet voices of summer once were.
Yet by the road where I see maidens fair
Tossing the ball, the bird's song is there !

Ah, could I slumber the winter away !
Wake I the while, I am wroth at his sway,
Which, far and wide, all the world must obey ;
Yet, troth, in time he'll be vanquished by May :
Then I'll pluck flowers, where frost lies to-day.

A DREAM'S INTERPRETATION

WHEN the summer-time was green,
 And the pretty flow'rs were seen
 Through the rich grass springing,
And the birds were singing,
Thither, where a fountain
Bubbles from the mountain,
By the forest murmuring,
Came I in my wandering
Where the nightingale did sing.

By the spring there stood a tree :
There a vision came to me.
I had come right early
To this fountain pearly,
Where the lime-tree's shadow
Falls athwart the meadow.
Down beside the spring I sat,
All my cares I straight forgat :
And slept sound because of that.

Then began I dream straightway
How all nations owned my sway ;
How my spirit, flinging
Off its weight, went winging

A DREAM'S INTERPRETATION

Heavenward, and flying,
Left my body lying.
Then had I surcease of pain :
Never shall I have, it's plain,
Such a glorious dream again.

Gladly had I slumbered on,
When the crows, with a malison
Woke me from my dreaming
With their cursèd screaming.
Would the fiend would take them
All to hell, and bake them !
For my dream they drove away :
Save that there no pebbles lay,
That had been their dying day.

Then a wondrous ancient dame,
Greatly to my comfort, came.
All my dream had told me
She began unfold me :
Here below I quote it,
That wise men may note it :
' One and two,' she said, ' are three !
And 'tis clear beside,' quoth she,
' That thy thumb a finger be ! '

WOMAN must ever be a woman's highest name,
  And worthier far than Lady, I should say.
  If some there be who of their womanhood
    think shame,
  Let them, before they choose, first mark this lay.
Ladies there are unwomanly ;
Of women none could say the same :
A woman's face is fair to see,
And fair to speak a woman's name.
However it with ladies fare,
Women the while all ladies are,
A mockery is doubtful praise,
As 'Ladyship' may be : but Womanhood is woman's
    crown always.

THE DECAY OF VIRTUE

SORROW left and pleasure fled :
    Who could bear the world for ever so?
    Save that it would seem ill-bred,
  I would cry out 'Ho, Fortune, ho!'
Ah, but Fortune will not hear!
Seldom will she venture near
To honest men.
If that be so, how shall I ever prosper then?

Alas! how little profits it,
    To judge from what I see before my eyes,
That I have wasted all my wit
    To honest ends, and cannot otherwise!
Honest and old-fashioned ways
Fare but badly in these days:
Very few
Win wealth and honour now, save those that evil do

That the men now act so ill
    Is all the women's fault, though this be sad.
While these cared for honour still,
    Through their favour all the world was glad.
How sweetly sounded then the praise
Those gave who marked their modest ways!
Now it is plain
That only with ill-doing we their love may gain.

For many ladies now I know
    In whom 'tis this that most doth grieve me:
The more the modesty I show,
    The less the honour that they give me.
Good breeding is what they despise.
With modest maids 'tis otherwise;
Not them I blame:
They blush for all that could put womanhood to shame.

Modest women, and good men,
    I bless them wheresoe'er they yet may be!
If I can serve their cause again,
    That will I do, that they may think of me.
But now the while I let them know
That, if the world no better grow,
My bread I'll make
As best I may, but song and singing I'll forsake!

NOR man nor maid may Love be named;
    Sans soul and body is it framed,
    Like is it to no mortal creature:
Men know its name, but not its nature;
And yet without it none may ever
Reach up to God Almighty's grace.

  .   .   .   .   .   .

Into false hearts it enters never.

THE POWER OF TRUE LOVE

TOO much in our brief life we meet
    Of Love that is but counterfeit.
    And yet I pledge my word that, where
One knows the coinage to be fair,
Though one went with it anywhither,
There were no evil end to fear.
True love to heaven is so near,
I pray that it may lead me thither.

D AME WORLD, the host I pray thee tell
       That now I owe him nothing more :
    For bed and board I've paid him well :
So let him strike me from his score.
Who owes him aught full well may sorrow :
Ere I would long be in his debt I'd turn me to a Jew, and
    borrow.
He will keep silence, till one day —
Then he will take the soul in pledge, if one have not the
    means to pay.

' Walter, thou hast no cause to chide !
    Remain awhile beside me still.
What hast thou asked that I denied ?
    Of honours thou hast had thy fill,
Which at thy prayer I gave to thee.
And far contenter had I been hadst thou more often
    begged of me.
Bethink thee well : Thy life is fair !
If thou indeed fall out with me, where wilt thou find
    content elsewhere ? '

Dame World, too long I've sucked of thee ;
   'Tis time that I at last were weaned !
Thy kisses nigh have ruined me,
   Though sweetest pleasure thence I gleaned :
For when I gazed into thine eyes,
The sight of thee was full of bliss ; 'twere false to say 'twas
    otherwise !
But, ah ! I saw so much of shame,
When thou didst turn thy back on me, that I must ever
    curse thy name.

' Then, since I cannot make thee stay,
   Do this one thing I ask of thee :
Think upon many a happy day ;
   And when the time hangs heavily,
Let thy looks sometimes linger here ! '
That would I wondrous gladly do, but that thy subtle
    snares I fear
Which none may flee that is thy guest.
Lady, God give you a good night ! I go to lay myself to
    rest.

GRANT me with joy to rise to-day,
Lord God, and go upon my way
Beneath Thy care, what path soe'er I take.
Lord Christ, vouchsafe in me to prove
The mighty power of Thy love,
And guard me well, for Thy sweet Mother's sake.
As Angels watched the Mother maid
And Thee within the manger laid,
Young child and ancient Deity,
Humble, with ox and ass on either hand,
Though Holy ~~Joseph~~ also kept Gabriel
His happy watch the while Ye slept,
And guarded You right faithfully:
So guard Thou me, that Thy divine command
May not be unfulfilled in me.

ON REINMAR'S DEATH

I

ALAS, that when the body dies
Man's wisdom and high qualities,
His youth and beauty, no one may inherit !
This well may be a wise man's thought,
Who sees the havoc death hath wrought.
Reinmar, with thee how much Art mourns of merit !
And justly shall it be tl.y lasting praise
That never one passed of thine earthly days
But thou didst tell of a good woman's grace and loveliness.
For this should they for ever thank thy tongue.
And had but this one line by thee been sung :
'Hail, Woman ! name of purest worth !' yet should all
women bless
Thy name for this, and pray for thine eternal happiness !

ON REINMAR'S DEATH

II

REINMAR, in truth I weep for thee
     Far more than thou hadst wept for me,
          If haply I had perished in thy stead.
I will confess it, on my faith :
Not for thy sake I mourn thy death,
     But that, with thee, thy noble art is dead.
To all the world thou lent'st thy joyous mood,
Striving to turn it to the love of good.
I sorrow for thine eloquent lips, and thy sweet gift of song :
That these, while I yet live, should silent grow.
Ah, hadst thou tarried but a while below !
I would have borne thee company : I shall not sing for
     long.
I pray thy soul may rest in peace ; and praise thee for thy
     tongue !

68

THE DAY OF JUDGMENT

AWAKE! The day is drawing near
　　　That well may fill all souls with fear,
　　　Whether they Christian, Jew, or heathen be!
We have beheld signs manifold
By which its coming is foretold,
As we in truth of Holy Writ may see.
The sun hath quenched its shining rays,
And treachery on all the ways
Scatters far and wide her seed :
The father by his children is betrayed,
His brother no one now believes,
Religion in its cowl deceives,
That heavenward our souls should lead ;
Force springs apace, while right and justice fade.
Awake! Ye give too little heed!

FRIENDS BEFORE KIN

To have few friends, but noble kin,
 Marry, small comfort lies therein !
 Friendship sans kindred were of greater worth.
For what avail is even royal birth
To those that wholly friendless are ?
Kinship's an honour all self-grown,
Friendship is won by worth alone.
Kin helps, but friendship's better far.

INCONSTANT FRIENDS

WHOEVER as a friend doth find
    Someone of such a constant mind
    That he remains unaltered to the end,
Let him with gladness cleave to such a friend.
As friends I oft have chosen such
As were so fickle and unstable,
To keep them I had been unable,
Had I desired it ne'er so much.

LIKE FOR LIKE

WHOE'ER as ice is slippery,
    And like a ball would handle me,
    If in his hands I slip and slide,
Let ro man me inconstant chide.
To faithful friends I too will stay
Ever four-square and balanced true,
But if their love should change its hue
For this and that, I roll away.

FALSE SMILES

GOD knows well, the Court should ever have my
praise
· When it the rules of courtesy at times obeys
In words, in honest counsel, and in courteous ways.
These grinning hypocrites who smile on me I scorn,
Whose tongues are honey, while their hearts are gall ;
A true friend's laugh should veil no wrong at all,
Purer than sunset glow foretelling the clear morn.
Now smile on me in deeds, or take your smiles elsewhere !
Let him who would deceive me, his false laughter spare ;
More for one honest ' Nay ' than two false ' Yeas ' I care !

VAULTING AMBITION

A SIX, by high ambition blinded,
 To be a Seven once was minded :
 Right sore it strove for this excessive station.
But he who leaves the road of moderation
Perchance will have to choose a path more straight.
Ambitious Six, thou'rt thrown as Three !
As Six there was a field for thee :
Now shrink into a Three's estate !

TO LEOPOLD OF AUSTRIA

CLOSED to me now is fortune's gate :
    Lo ! orphan-like, outside I wait,
      And all my knocking helps me not a whit.
What greater marvel could there be ?
The rain falls on all sides of me,
    Yet I receive no single drop of it.
The largess spent by Austria's lord,
Like sweetest rain from heaven poured,
The people blesses and the land.
He is a meadow fair and gay,
Where flowers may be culled in sheaves :
Ah ! if but one among the leaves
He'd pluck me with his lavish hand,
I'd praise the happy fortune of that day.
Let this remind him how I stand !

A CHANGE OF FORTUNE

WHEN it to Frederick of Austria did betide
   That he his soul did save, the while his body
   died,
My crane-like steps were hid with him in earth.
Then crawled I like a peacock wheresoe'er I went,
Down to my very knees my head I humbly bent.
But now I hold it high, as suits my worth :
Of fire and hearth I now am free,
For Crown and Empire to themselves have welcomed me.
Ho ! then, whoe'er would tread a merry measure !
Now am I rid of all my care :
At last along an even pathway I may fare,
And mount once more into a dream of pleasure.

NOTE.—Cast adrift by the death of Frederick of Austria, Walter seems to
have passed through a time of want and anxiety, as, apart from this poem, his
eager appeals to Duke Leopold show. The 'Crown and Empire' refers to
Philip of Suabia, whose cause·Walter continued to support, doubtless not
without return, until the Emperor's tragic death.

HOST AND GUEST

TO KING FREDERICK

'WELCOME, sir host!' such greeting none may
now allow me :
'Welcome, sir guest!' and I must humbly
render thanks and bow me.
Host and home are both right honourably named :
Guest and lodging ofttimes make one sore ashamed.
Ah, might I but receive a guest, and take
As host the bows that he would have to make !
'Stay here to-night ! To-morrow fare !'—what juggler's
life is this ?
' I am at home' or ' I will home,' marry, were less amiss !
Guests and Check small welcome have, y-wis !
Save me from my guestship, Sire, that God save you from
Check !

TO KING FREDERICK

ROME'S Lord, Apulia's King, have pity upon me,
  Who, rich in art, am yet thus plunged in
    poverty.
By my own hearth I long to sit, might it but be!
Ho! how I then would sing of wild birds as of yore,
Of heather and of flowers how I then would sing!
How sweetly would fair ladies thank me when I bring
The glow of rose and lily to their cheeks once more.
Now I come late, and early ride: a guest, alas!
Let them who have a home sing of the flowers and grass.
Relieve my need, most gracious King, that your own need
  may pass.

• *THE FIEF*

I HAVE my fief! I have my fief! All men give ear!
   Of chilblains on my feet I now have little fear,
   And will no longer beg of lords who will not hear.
The noble King, the generous King, has dealt with me
So that in winter I have warmth, in summer air.
Now to my neighbours I appear by far more fair:
No more they'll see me like a ghost, as formerly.   *see below*
Sans fault of mine I have been poor by far too long,
My breath was foul with much complaining of my wrong:
That hath the King made sweet again, and sweet my
      song.

A FIEF of thirty marks gave me the King my lord,
But little, none the less, is there for me to hoard,
Nor yet, for sending over sea, to set on board.
For though the name be great, the nut is yet so small
That I can neither hold, nor hear, nor mark it :
How should I then in ships or boats embark it ?
Shall I then hold to it, my friends, or let it fall ?
For all the priests' contentions care I not a pin !
They'll never search in coffers where there's naught to win.
Well, let them search and search in mine.   There's not a
    coin therein.

[1] This is evidently intended as a half humorous address to the priests who were collecting money for the Crusades.   Elsewhere Walter had openly enough expressed his doubts as to the actual destination of the fund.   Here he contents himself with pleading the poverty of his fief as a reason for not contributing.

LORD GOD, whoever thinks not shame
    Thy ten commandments to proclaim,
    And yet to break them, can of love know naught.
  ' Our Father ' many pray to Thee
  Who yet my brothers will not be,
And these speak weighty words with little thought.
  Of the same stuff God made us all :
The food we eat is bitten small
Between our teeth, whate'er it be.
And who may tell the master from the man,
Though he them both in life had known,
When, poor remains of ash and bone,
Worms feast upon them equally ?
To serve Him who sustains this wondrous plan
Christians, Jews, and heathen all agree.

THE INHOSPITABLE CLOISTER [1]

OF Tegernsee they oft declare
　　One finds good entertainment there :
　　A mile then from my road I thither turned.
I am a man of wondrous sense
To doubt my own experience,
And trust so much what I from strangers learned.
I blame them not—God grant us both His grace !
They gave me water in the cloister :
So that moister
I left the abbot's table, and the place.

---

[1] The celebrated Benedictine Abbey of Tegernsee was situated on the lake
of that name in Upper Bavaria.　It was founded A.D. 736, and suppressed
A.D. 1804.

THE DECAY OF COURTESY

WHO now shall shine in honour's hall?
The young knights' chivalry is small,
And squires now flaunt their boorishness
In word and action, unashamed.
Virtue as folly now is blamed.
Look, how ill customs spring and spread apace!
There was a time one whipped the young
Who kept no curb upon their tongue;
Now it is held a gentle art
To shout, and slander each pure woman's name.
Now woe betide your hides and hair,
Who never for a pleasure care,
Unless it break a woman's heart!
Lo! thus we see sin side by side with shame,
In which too many have a part.

TO THE YOUNG

NOW curb your pace, and have a care, young people
   all !
   If ye give rein to your desires, ye'll have a fall ;
The thought of gold within your hearts too much ye
   treasure.
There [1] that will be a lasting pain, though here it yield you
   pleasure !
Drive out your base desires with honest thoughts always ;
Love God, and He will send you happy days ;
Strive for good fame with might, if ye true joy would
   reach ;
Never put trust in those who evil maxims teach ;
Believe whate'er of good the priests may preach.
And, if ye would turn all to gold, then speak in woman's
   praise !

[1] dort. *Cf.* Greek ἐν τῷ ἐκεῖ, *i.e.* in the next world.

V .

WEALTH MORE THAN HONOUR

RIGHT through the world I've travelled now from
Mur to Seine ;
And well I know, from Po to Trave, the ways of
men ;
The most part reck not by what means their wealth they
reap.
If in such wise I win it, then, chivalry, go to sleep !
Wealth was ever welcome, yet was honour's state
Higher by far ; now is wealth grown so great
Honour must stand aside, while it to ladies' favour presses,
And part with princes at Kings' council boards possesses !
Woe to thee, Wealth ! Thy curse it is distresses
The state of Rome ; and in our shame thy share is far too
great.

W E'RE troubled by a certain set :
    If these but forth were cast,
    A man of worth and honest grit
At court might raise his head.
He ne'er had chance to speak as yet.
They wag their jaws so fast
That, were he blest with finest wit,
'Twould serve him not a shred :
' I, and this donkey here,
Will bray into his ear,
That not in choir ye'll hear
A monk as loudly roar ! '
Sensible talk always
Should meet with honest praise :
But when a donkey brays—
Enough !   I'll say no more !

TO THE ARCHANGELS [1]

HE who ne'er Himself began,
   Yet make begin both will and can,
   Can make an end as well, and without end.
Since all creation to His Will must bend,
Can there be praise more high than He inspires?
First, then, to Him my song I raise
Whose praise is higher than all praise;
And holy is the praise that He requires.

Now praise we too the sweetest maid
Who to her Son ne'er vainly prayed.
Mother of Him she is who saved us all.
What fairer comfort on our souls could fall
Than that all heaven her will obeys?
Come then the old and eke the young
That her high glory may be sung!
Since she is good, she's good to praise!

[1] See the Introduction.

I ought to greet you angels too,

But that I'm far too wise to do:

What to the heathen have ye wrought of ill?

Since all unseen ye are and voiceless still,

Tell us, to help the work, what have ye done?

If silently I too could wreak

God's vengeance, think not I would speak:

I'd leave you gentlemen alone![1]

Sir Michäel, Sir Gabriel,

Sir foe of devils Raphael,

Wisdom is yours, and strength, and art of healing;[2]

And three angelic hosts behind you wheeling

Haste to obey your orders joyfully.

If you want praise, then show some sense!

The heathen mock your impotence:

Praised I you now, they'd mock at me!

---

[1] Ich wolte iuch hêrren ruowen lân.

[2] Wisdom is the attribute of Gabriel, strength of Michäel, and the power of healing that of Raphael. This attack on the angels, which Herr Wilmanns seems, hardly I think with justice, to regard as a somewhat ribald jest, was not without precedent. St. Bernard had declaimed against those who thought that God should himself rescue the Holy Land: the repeated failures of the Christians were, he said, intended as a trial of faith and a moral discipline; and Innocent III., in his Encyclical of A.D. 1213, refers to the same matter in somewhat similar terms. See Wilm. II., 283.

A JOYLESS TIME

WHAT use in tender rhyming? What in singing?
What use in wealth? In woman's loveliness?
Since all delight the world aside is flinging,
And wrong is wrought and suffered sans redress ;
Since honour, kindness, faith, and self-respect
Are fallen in neglect,
Hearts, joyous once, are turned to heaviness.

√

PAST AND PRESENT

ALAS, my happy years! Whither are they sped?
Was, then, my life a fact, or but a vision fled?
And was that but a dream that I so real thought?
It seems that I have lain asleep, and knew it not.
I am awakened now, and no more understand
What once I knew as clearly as my own right hand.
People and countryside which as a child I knew,
All strange are grown to me, as though it were untrue.
Those who my playmates were are aged now and cold,
Ploughed up are now the fields, and stripped are wood
    and wold.
Save that the brooks are flowing, as they used to flow,
My sorrow nevermore would any solace know.
Coldly they greet me now who knew me well of old,
The world is full of sadness and troubles manifold:
And fancy bears me back to many a happy day
Which, like a ripple in the sea, long since has passed away,
For evermore, alas!

Alas !　How grave and sad young people now are grown !
Those who in days of old no care or pain had known
Do little now but weep.　Alas, how should that be ?
Wherever now I turn, no happiness I see.
Dancing, laughter, song, for grief are all forgot :
Never yet Christian man saw such a woeful lot.
Mark how poorly now ladies are garlanded ;
In raiment fit for boors proud knights are habited :
From Rome have come to us letters grim and sad :
Sorrow indeed we may, but nevermore be glad.
It makes my heart so sad (we lived so well of yore),
That now I needs must weep who used to laugh before ;
The wild birds in the wood droop at our bitter plaint :
What wonder, then, that I should feel my courage faint ?
What am I saying, fool !　I pray to be forgiven,
For those who seek joy here will lose the joy of Heaven
For evermore, alas !

Alas ! though things be fair, poison is in them all :
E'en in the honey-pot I see the hidden gall.
The world is gay without, white, and red, and green,
But sombre as the grave and dark as death within.
Let him whom she beguiled his comfort now behold :
A penance small may shrive sins great and manifold.

Bethink you well, Sir Knights, to you is the appeal :
Bright helmets ye do wear, and shining rings of steel,
Firm shields are on your arms, and hallowed swords ye
    bear !
Would God that I myself your victory might share !
Then, needy as I am, I'd earn me richest pay—
Not gold, nor gifts of land, nor glittering array ;
But that eternal crown I evermore would wear,
Which any churl may win with shield and sword and
    spear !
If on this journey blest I oversea might pass
I'd sing for evermore ' Praise God,' and nevermore ' Alas !'
Nevermore ' Alas ! '

POLITICAL POEMS

I

I SAT one day alone
Crosslegged upon a stone,
With elbow resting on my knee,
And chin and cheek reflectively
Supported in my hand,
And tried to understand
Why we are called on earth to live.
And little comfort could I give
How three things we should cherish
So that not one might perish :
Honour and worldly wealth are two,
Harm oft from each to other grew ;
The third is Heaven's grace,
Which takes the foremost place.
In one shrine would I set the three.
Alas ! it nevermore may be

That honour and wealth shall dwell,
With Heaven's grace as well,
Together in one heart again;
All roads and paths from them are ta'en;
Falsehood in ambush lurks;
Violence vaunts its works;
Justice and peace are wounded sore;
If these two be not quickly healed,
　the three will never prosper more!

II

I heard a fountain brimming,
And watched the fishes swimming;
And marked what in the world did pass,
Forest and field, rush, leaf, and grass,
All things that fly and creep,
And beasts that run and leap,
And saw that of all forms of life,
Not one there is lives free from strife:
Wild beasts and creeping things
Have all their quarrellings;
The birds, too, fight right angrily.
Yet in one thing they all agree—
That none would live content
Had they no Government.

They choose them Kings to make awards,
And some are vassals, some are lords.
Then, wretched Germany!
How ill it fares with thee!
Since every insect has its King,
While all thine honour's perishing.
Turn ere it be too late!
The princes grow too great;
These threadbare Kinglets press thee sore:
Crown Philip with the Kaiser's crown,
    and bid them vex thy peace no more.

III

I saw with mine own eyes
The whole world's mysteries;
Since I beheld, and also heard,
What all men wrought in deed and word:
At Rome I heard them lie,
And cheat two Kings thereby;[1]
Whence there arose a direr war
Than ever was on earth before;

[1] *I.e.*, Otho of Brunswick and Philip of Suabia, the rival claimants.
'Pope Innocent III., in the affair of the election to the German Empire,
played so diplomatic a game that, as he himself writes, till the spring of
1199 both Kings could boast of his favour, and in Germany it was loudly
declared that his aim was not the welfare, but the degradation and ruin of the
Empire.'

When priests and laity

Began their rivalry,

A woe that was both sore and great :

Body and soul lay desolate.

The parsons fought right well,

Yet could they not prevail.

The sword and spear then laid they down,

And took again to stole and gown ;

They damned all those they would,

And no one whom they should ;

In God's Church thus they havoc wrought.

Far in a cloister cell methought

I heard a hermit [1] weep

In anguish great and deep ;

He cried to God, 'Thy Kingdom come !'

Alas! the Pope is far too young ; [2]

in mercy help thy Christendom !

[1] This 'hermit,' who is mentioned several times, is probably a type of those priests who were loyal to the Empire ; but some characteristic German controversy has raged round the question of his identity.

[2] Pope Innocent III. was, at the date of his election, A.D. 1198, only 37 years old, a fact which was held by his opponents to explain his ambitious schemes and vigorous attacks on the secular power. The meaning of this line may, however, be that Walter, at this early stage of the struggle, wishes to blame, not the Pope, but his advisers. The princes assembled at Bamberg, in their letter of protest, had laid the responsibility, not on the Pope, but on the legates (Wilmanns, I., 96).

98

KING PHILIP'S CORONATION

AT Magdeburg there walked, upon that happy morn
    When, of a maid whom he for mother chose, was
    born

Our blessed Lord, Philip the handsome King.

There walked a Kaiser's brother and a Kaiser's son

Beneath one robe, three titles and yet one !

The Empire's crown and sceptre carrying,

Gently he stepped, for he had little haste ;

Behind him came his queen, high-born and chaste,

A rose without a thorn, a dove devoid of gall.

When was such ~~loyalty~~ elsewhere? *breeding*

Saxons and Thuringians did homage there :

In wise men's eyes naught fairer could befall.

NOTE.—The coronation of Philip of Suabia took place at Magdeburg on Christmas Day, A.D. 1199. His queen, the beautiful and gentle Irene, was a Greek princess, daughter of the Emperor Isaac Angelus, and had once been married, or at least betrothed, to Roger, son and colleague of Tancred, the last of the Norman line of Sicilian kings. After the death of Roger and of Tancred, and the sudden and tragic overthrow of their house by the Emperor Henry VI., Irene had been left helpless and friendless, until Philip of Suabia, the future Emperor, captivated by her beauty and charm, made her his wife. Her amiable and sweet nature may have had its share in securing the success of Philip's efforts against the unpopular Otho, for Walter von der Vogelweide, in applying to the Empress attributes usually reserved for the Blessed Virgin, was but giving voice to universal popular sentiment.

99

TO KING PHILIP

KING PHILIP, they complain that see thee near
    That thou art niggard of thy thanks. From this
    I fear
That thou the more wilt lose in other ways.
Better, with grace, a thousand pounds bestow
Than thirty thousand without thanks. Thou dost not
    know
How one with gifts may honour win and praise.
Think how well Saladin could give :
Formed should a King's hands be, said he, like any sieve ;
For thus a ruler wins both fear and love.
To him of England, too, give heed,
At what a cost he, through his open hand, was freed.
One loss is good that two-fold gain shall prove.

NOTE.—The remark attributed here to Saladin (died A.D. 1193) is nowhere else mentioned in history ; but his generosity and high-mindedness had become proverbial in Europe. Of the reputation of Richard Cœur de Lion ('he of England') for generosity less is known. The ransom demanded by Leopold of Austria was 150,000 marks, an enormous sum for those days. Perhaps Walter had the story of the faithful minstrel, Blondel, in his mind ; and, ascribing his devotion to the generous way in which he had been treated by his master, uses the incident as a delicate hint to King Philip. ·

TO THE EMPEROR OTHO

LORD KAISER, I a welcome bring.
No more you bear the name of King :
For higher than all crowns your crown has soared !
Blessing and strength are in your hand,
And good and ill, at your command,
Are ready or for vengeance or reward.
And this I tell you too :
The princes your return awaited
Right loyally, obedient to your sway ;
And Meissen's lord is true,
Nor e'er his loyalty abated :
God's angel sooner had been led astray.

NOTE. —After the final rupture between Innocent III. and the Emperor Otho
(A.D. 1211) certain princes of the Empire, with the King of Bohemia, the
Landgrave of Thuringia, and the Archbishop of Mainz at their head, met at
Nuremberg, and there drew up a formal invitation to Frederick of Sicily to
come forward as a candidate for the crown. The return of Otho put a stop
for the time to the plans of the conspirators ; and at the great court which
the Emperor held at Frankfort on Palm Sunday, A.D. 1212, most of them put
in an appearance, among others the Margrave of Meissen, in whose service
Walter would seem, at this time, to have been. It was on this occasion that
the above song was composed. Whether it had any effect in allaying the sus-
picions of the Emperor may be doubted : it protested, perhaps, too much.
Circumstances, however, forced Otho to adopt a conciliatory attitude, for the
Margrave's help was necessary to him at any cost. But the latter, in spite of
the favourable terms which had been paid for his support, did not long remain
faithful to the Emperor's cause ; for the very next year he is found among the
adherents of Frederick. In the meantime, however, Walter von der Vogelweide had himself transferred his allegiance to the Hohenstaufen
(Wilm. I., 110).

EAGLE AND LION

TO THE EMPEROR OTHO IV

LORD KAISER, when you, by the cord,
 To Germany have peace restored,
  From foreign tongues your praises you will
   hear.
This, with small trouble, you'll attain,
And Christendom unite again,
 To your own glory, and the heathen's fear.
You bear two Cæsars' might :
The eagle's virtue, and the lion's strength :
These two emblazoned are upon your shield.
Would that the twain would fight
As comrades, and the heathen force at length
To strength and generosity to yield ![1]

---

[1] Strength was supposed to be the characteristic quality of the lion, generosity of the eagle, which, according to the legend, always left a part of its prey for the benefit of smaller birds.

A DIVINE MESSAGE[1]

LORD KAISER, as God's herald here,
   Bringing a message, I draw near:
   Thou rul'st the earth, the heavens He.
This plaint He sends (His steward thou),
That the blaspheming heathens now
In His Son's land defy both Him and thee.
   Do not His cause forget!
His Son, whose name is Christ, bade say
That He in judgment would reward you well
(Now place Him in thy debt!)
When He is steward, on That Day,
And should you plead against the Fiend in Hell!

[1] From the similarity of form, and especially of the opening address, this poem would seem to have been sung on the same occasion as the last two. It has, however, been argued that this was hardly the time for a call to the Emperor to go on crusade, since his presence was so urgently needed in Germany, and he was, moreover, under sentence of excommunication. The taking of the cross, however, by no means involved an immediate fulfilment of the vow, and the hostility of the Pope would weigh little with those who affected at least to see in the attitude of the Holy See the main obstacle to the attainment of what all Christendom so ardently desired.

TO POPE INNOCENT III

ON THE EXCOMMUNICATION OF OTHO IV., AFTER HIS
INVASION OF APULIA, IN NOVEMBER, A.D. 1210

L ORD POPE, my soul's defence shall be
    That I am but obeying thee.
      To Christendom we heard you give the word
How we to Cæsar should behave
When you to him God's blessing gave—
    That we should kneel to him and hail him lord ![1]
Also remember well,
You said : ' Let him that blesses thee
Be blest, and he that curses thee be curst
With curses terrible ! '
'Fore God, then, if priests' honour be
Your care, of this bethink you first.

[1] Otho IV. was solemnly crowned and anointed as Emperor, in St. Peter's at Rome, by Innocent III., on October 4, A.D. 1209. (See Raumer, *Hohen-staufen*, Bd. iii., p. 9.)

TO THE PRIESTS

GOD gives us whom He will for King;
    This sets me not a-marvelling:
        We laymen marvel at the priests alone.
A short while since they used to teach
What now as damnable they preach.
    Now let them but, for God's sake and their own,
Tell us, by all that's true,
Which doctrine we are cheated by:
Let them take one, and well enlarge on it,
Be it the old or new!
For one, we hold, must be a lie:
Into one mouth two tongues but badly fit.

N OW is the See of Rome in far more evil case
  Than when the wizard Gerbert sat in Peter's
    place,
Since none, save he himself, through him to hell did come,
While this one damns, besides himself, all Christendom ;
So that all tongues cry out to Heaven, and weep,
Asking the Lord how long He yet will sleep.
They set at naught His Will, and falsify His Word ;
His Treasurer steals from the heavenly hoard ;
His Vicar robs, and slays with fire and sword ;
His Shepherd is become a wolf among his sheep.

NOTE.—Pope Innocent III. is compared with Sylvester II., formerly named
Gerbert, who occupied the Papal See from 999–1003. Sylvester had distinguished himself by his great and many-sided learning, and especially by his
knowledge of mathematics and natural science. Of his magic art the genera-
tions nearest to him knew nothing ; at most it was whispered mysteriously
that Gerbert had acquired his learning among the Saracens of Spain. The
first traces of the legend (of his having sold his soul to the devil) are found at
the end of the eleventh century ; in William of Malmesbury it is fully developed, and at the beginning of the twelfth century its truth is not disputed ;
and it is widely spread in chronicles, legends, and collections of curious lore.
Heretical sects dated the decay of the Roman Church from Pope Sylvester, by
whom it had been infected with evil. This was the teaching of the Waldenses
and Cathari (Wilm., p. 319, note I., 214.). See also *inter alia* Milman's
Latin Christianity, vol. iii., p. 348. Gerbert would seem to have invented,
among other things, an organ worked by steam !

EVIL EXAMPLE

WE all make moan—yet know not what it is that
grieves us—
That 'tis the Pope himself, our father, who
deceives us.
Oh! in how fatherly a way he now precedes us!
We follow in his steps, whithersoe'er he leads us.
Now, all the world, to what I blame in this give heed:
If he be greedy, all men ape his greed:
If he tell lies, his lies they all repeat ;
If he deceive, they join in his deceit.
Mark well, whoever thinks my words unmeet—
In this wise this new Judas will as the old one speed.

THE SEDUCER

YE bishops and ye noble priests, ye go astray ;
 For see, with Satan's cords the Pope leads
  you away !
Holds he St. Peter's Keys, as ye are always preaching,
Then say why from his books he blots St. Peter's teach-
  ing !
To buy and sell what God has freely given
Forbidden is by all our hopes of heaven.
Now from his black book let him learn it, which from hel¹
The devil sent him, and seek there a spell.
Ye cardinals, ye gild your chancels well :
But our old altar now by storm and rain is riven.

NOTE. — This poem, denouncing the sale of Indulgences, is addressed to the
higher German clergy, as opposed to the cardinals, *i.e.*, the Roman clergy,
who gild and enrich their churches at the expense of the German Church.
'Here the poet's arrows hit real abuses in the Church ; but Innocent himself
recognised them as such, and was striving to reform them. A year before his
death, at the great Council in Rome, the exaggerated and ill-timed use of
Indulgences . . . was pointedly forbidden. At times the secular princes
pressed the Church to make more effective use of the means at her disposal.
The freethinking Emperor Frederick II. complains to the Pope that the
preachers of the crusade granted *no* Indulgences ' (Wilmanns, p. 114).

THE POPE'S APOSTASY

IF heart there be that, in these days, turns not to sin,
    God's love and blessed spirit surely dwells therein,
    Since 'tis the Pope himself who misbelief now breeds!
Now mark ye of what sort are now priests' words and
    deeds.
Their acts and doctrine once from wrong were free :
But now, if they in word and works agree,
'Tis that we hear those speak, and see those working ill,
Who should our souls with good examples fill.
Well may we simple laity despair :
And my good hermit,[1] too, our grief and tears shall share.

[1] See note on p. 98.

THE FOREIGN CHEST

AHA! how Christianly the Pope of us makes mock,
When what he here hath wrought he tells his
foreign flock.

What he thus says, he never even should have thought:

Says he: 'Beneath one crown two Germans have I
brought,

That they the realm may burn, and wreck, and waste;

Their wealth the while into my chests I cast.

I've cudgelled them with my good stick,[1] their wealth will
all be mine,

Their German silver flows into my Roman shrine.

Now feast, ye priests, on fowls and drink your wine,

And let the witless German laymen . . . fast!'

[1] The stick, with which the Pope is here said to cudgel the Germans, is the
'Opferstock,' *i.e.* collecting-box, mentioned again in the next poem, a play
on words which cannot be rendered into English. This poem belongs to the
year 1213. Simrock (ii. 145), speaking of it, says: 'The year before, Innocent,
with a view to furthering the Crusades, directed that collecting-boxes (truncos)
were to be set up in all the churches, in order to gather contributions for the
recovery of the Holy Land. The box was to have three locks, and the keys
of them were to be entrusted to a priest, a layman, and a member of a religious
order; but the money was to be applied at the discretion of those who should
be appointed for that purpose. Walter, however, sees in this arrangement
nothing but avarice: the Pope only desired to fill his coffers with German
silver.' See also Wilmanns, I., p. 112.

SIR BOX, now tell us, has the Pope but sent you
hither
　　That you may fatten him, while Germans pine and
wither?
When, brimful, to the Lateran you come once more,
He will but play on us the same old trick he played
before :
He'll tell us then, how rent the Empire must remain,
Till all the churches fill his chests again.
Little, methinks, of all this silver in God's cause is spent :
To part with a great treasure priests are ill content.
Sir Box, for mischief you are hither sent,
To find how many fools among us Germans yet remain.

NOTE.—Besides taking the measures mentioned on the preceding page,
Innocent, for the purposes of the Crusade, had imposed upon himself and the
cardinals a tax of a tenth of their income, and upon all other ecclesiastics one
of a fortieth. ' There can be no question that, in this affair, Innocent was in
holy earnest!' (Wilmanns, I., p. 112).

THE PRIESTS' ELECTION[1]

KING CONSTANTINE did once bestow
These gifts, as I would have you know,
Upon the See of Rome: spear, cross and
crown.
At once the angel loudly cried,
'Woe, woe! a threefold woe betide!
Till now the Church hath lived in fair renown.
Now poison in her cup doth fall,
Her honey mingled is with gall:
This to the world a curse shall be!'
All other princes now in honour dwell,
Only the highest counts as naught.
This hath the priests' election wrought.
Sweet God! our cry goes up to Thee.
The priests would steal the laymen's rights as well:
The angel warned us truthfully.

[1] According to O. Abel (quoted by Pfeiffer) this rhyme belongs to the
years 1212-1215, when Innocent III. was at the zenith of his power, and
Walter von der Vogelweide was still on the side of Otho IV. against
Frederick II., who was at that time called contemptuously the 'Priests' King'
by his opponents.

NOTE.—'Like the majority of his contemporaries, Walter believes in the historical truth of the Donation of Constantine ; and the only doubts he has are as to the nature and scope of the gift. While the friends of the temporal power of the Church maintained that the Imperial insignia and the Western Empire had been bestowed by Constantine on the See of Rome, and argued from this that the Emperor was to be regarded as a vassal of the Pope, holding his dignity but as a feudatory of the Church, others saw in such claims a disturbance of the Divine order of the world ; for the Pope had received from God, not the keys of this world, but those of the other. Innocent III. naturally asserted the extreme view : " Omne regnum Occidentis ei (Silvestro) tradidit et dimisit." It is this claim that Walter here opposes. The scope of the Donation he limits to a minimum : Constantine had given to the Pope not the Imperium itself, but only the insignia of Empire. The Imperium the King receives by the election of the princes.' (Wilm., I., p. 245.)

THE JUGGLER

SOME lords there are I know, like jugglers, under-
    stand
    How to deceive and trick with cunning sleight of
    hand ;
They cry : ' Beneath this hat what think you ye will see ? '
Now lift it up ! There stands a wild hawk in its bravery.
Lift it again : it now a peacock proud will be ;
Once more : and lo ! a monster from the sea.
Yet, change it ne'er so oft, at last 'tis but a sorry crow.
My friend, I know the trick ! Ho, ho ! Ha, ha ! Ho, ho !
Keep to thyself thy lying juggler's show !
I'd break it o'er thy head, were I thy match in size !
Thou blowest too much dust into my eyes ;
Unless thou guard me from such tricky lies,
No more I'll work the bellows in thy company.

NOTE.—This poem is directed against the Emperor Otho IV. and his habit
of making promises which he was either unable or unwilling to fulfil. Matthew
Paris calls Otho ' magnificus promissor et parcissimus exhibitor.'

THE CHAMELEON[1]

A MIGHTY wonder in the world of late I've seen
    Which, even in the sea, a monster strange had
        been:
Because of this, my joy is dulled, and all my grief grown
    keen.
Like is it to an evil man. If one but hold
His laughter to the touchstone, it proves counterfeit.
He bites, ere ever snarl betrays his bitter hate;
Within his jaws two tongues there are, that now are hot,
    now cold;
In his sweet honey there lies hid a venomous nail,
His cloudless laughter brings a storm of stinging hail;
When one finds him out, he turns, and shows his scorpion's
    tail.

[1] Pfeiffer thinks that this allegory is a thinly disguised attack on Otho IV.

THE WAY TO DRINK[1]

HIS drinking who drinks overmuch I blame.
   How looks an honourable man whose tongue
      is lame
With wine? With sin, methinks, he decks himself and
   shame.   .
Better it would beseem him could he use his feet
So as to stand without a prop where people are.
How soft soe'er he's carried, better he walked by far.
To quench his thirst let each man drink then what is
   meet :
Nor mortal sin nor shame from moderation flows.
But he who drinks so that he no more knows
Himself nor God, God's high commandments overthrows.

[1] This poem forms one of a series directed against the Emperor Otho IV.

YE princes, who would gladly rid you of the King,
    Follow my counsel: I propose no foolish
    thing.

To Trani, aye and far beyond, I'd send him journeying.

In Christ's high cause he arms, and they that him prevent,

In God's despite and that of Christendom, do mortal sin.

Let him, ye enemies, his enterprise begin :

What if he ne'er return to stir your discontent ?

If, which may God forfend, he stay away, laugh ye !

But ours, if he come home to us, the laugh shall be.

The upshot let us both await ; and take this rede from me !

NOTE.—As early as the twenty-fifth of July, 1215, the Emperor Frederick II.
had taken the cross, on the occasion of his coronation at Aix. All manner of
hindrances had, however, hitherto prevented him from starting for the Holy
Land. At the beginning of A.D. 1220 he held diets at Augsburg and
Nuremberg, and received the oaths of the princes and nobles that they would
follow him. These were, however, so lukewarm in the cause and so dis-
affected to himself that he wrote to the Pope, Honorius III., that he could
not trust them to follow if he went first. How he subsequently started, was
forced by sickness to return, and was excommunicated, are matters of history.
Trani was the port in Southern Italy whence the Crusaders usually set out.

M Y ancient eremite, of whom I sang before,
 What time the former Pope[1] vexed and
  oppressed us sore,

Lest its lords prove weak, fears for the Church of God once
 more.

If thus the bad are praised by them, saith he, and good
 men banned,

They'll find themselves repaid in kind, e'er many days are
 o'er :

It well may be they'll lose their livings and their land :

Many armed knights there are among that loyal band

To whom the empire owes reward, who now expectant
 stand.

---

[1] *I.e.* Innocent III , by his excommunication of Philip of Suabia. This
poem was composed after the excommunication of Frederick II. by Pope
Gregory IX. (A. D. 1227), and is a warning to the German prelates not to fall
away from the Emperor. In Apulia, at least, the threats here thrown out were
acted on, and all priests who obeyed the interdict were deprived of their
livings ; though even Frederick II. seems never to have gone so far as to act
on the suggestion above made, to confiscate the lands of the Church for the
benefit of his lay followers, though this idea would seem to have been seriously
mooted by Otho IV. (Wilm. I., p. 115.)

ON THE DEATH OF ARCHBISHOP ENGELBERT

ARCHBISHOP ENGELBERT of Cologne, chancellor of the empire, and one of Walter's most generous patrons, had at the end of 1220 and beginning of 1221 been appointed by the Emperor, Frederick II., regent of the empire, and governor of his young son, King Henry VII., during the Emperor's absence in Italy. During the tenure of this office the Archbishop signalised himself by his stern and ruthless suppression of disorder and lawlessness, and by his endeavour to reduce the turbulent and powerful feudal nobles to obedience. To the bitter hatred aroused by this policy he fell a victim, being murdered, November 7, 1225, by his own nephew, Count Frederick of Isenburg. In the following lines, Walter, in giving vent to his own grief and indignation at this treacherous and unnatural crime, expresses also the popular feeling of the time.

Engelbert was at once regarded by the people as a martyr, and in due course venerated as a saint. His murderer, after eluding for a year the pursuit of justice, was finally caught, and broken on the wheel ; a punishment which Walter thinks quite inadequate.

HIS life I praised, his death I evermore will plain.
Woe to him who this noble prince of Köln hath slain !
Alas, that earth should have his burden to sustain !
No torture, to his guilt proportioned, can I find him :
A hempen cord about his neck were far too mild a pain,

Nor would I burn, nor tear him limb from limb, nor blind
   him,

Nor yet would break him on the wheel, nor on it bind
   him :

I wait for hell, while yet he lives, to gape and close
   behind him !

TO KING HENRY VII

THOU self-willed boy, grown art thou too awry
    Since none there is can set thee straight
    (Pity that for the rod too big thou art,
For swords as yet too small!).
Well sleep now, and thy pleasure take!
A silly simpleton, methinks, was I
Ever to hold thy worth so great.
Thy wantonness I hid within my heart,
Reckt not of wrongs at all,
And broke my back all for thy sake.
I give thee up, and in my stead
Thy school may now be masterless.
If thou reap good from someone else
I shall rejoice at his success.
But well I know that when his force
Comes to an end, his skill alone
Will little progress make.

NOTE.—This poem has given rise to considerable controversy. By many it has been held sufficient proof of Walter's appointment as tutor to the young king (*cf.* Pfeiffer, p. 283). In the absence of any historical confirmation of so remarkable a fact, other and more plausible explanations have been offered.

During his absence in the Holy Land the Emperor Frederick II. had appointed a council of regency, with Duke Ludwig of Bavaria at its head, to assist the young king in the government of Germany. But Henry was head-strong, and had moreover his own theories of government, which by no means tallied with the plans of his father. He soon quarrelled with Duke Ludwig, alienated all the more powerful secular princes of the empire, and finally broke also with the great ecclesiastics, who for a time had supported him. Yet there seems to have been method in his madness; for, relying on the support of the lower nobility and the cities, he carried on a successful war against Duke Ludwig, and his career of victory was only stopped by the unexpected return of the Emperor.

The above poem is placed by Wilmanns in the year 1228, at Christmas, when Ludwig left Henry's court. It is the Duke, not Walter, who gives Henry up. 'The attitude of the regent would have given Walter his cue; and his rhyme was not so much the expression of his own feelings as of those of the government of the empire' (See Wilm., I., p. 151).

LOW-BORN COUNSELLORS

WHEN the high-born by the base
  Are ousted, and these to their place
  Are upward forced, the court has little gain.
How should a man that hath no skill
Counsel otherwise than ill ?
Shall he heal me where I feel no pain ?
The high-born now are thrust without the gate,
The while the low are called to rule the State :
These, when their shallow wits run dry, mark you, can do
 no more
Than straight betake themselves to trickeries ;
These to the princes they will teach, and lies.
'Tis these that rob our honour, and upon our rights make
 war :
Look now, how low the Crown is brought, and the Church
 stricken sore.

NOTE.—This poem is directed against the action of King Henry VII. in
quarrelling with the greater princes, and resting on the support of the lower
nobles and the retainers of the house of Staufen. See note to the preceding
poem.

IN wonder through the world I strayed,
Till wondrous things grew all too plain :
Alas ! The thrones I found unoccupied
Where wisdom, age, and nobleness
Once sat in mighty state.

Help, Mary's Son ! Help, Mother Maid,
These three to their true place again !
Let them not throneless all too long abide !
Their manifold and deep distress
Leaves my heart desolate.

Their threefold throne, their titles three
Upstart folly holdeth now.
Alas, that we who served the three
To such a one as this must bow !
So justice halts, and virtue pines, and sickens shame.
That is my plaint : Woe's me ! 'tis not too great !

FULL ofttimes have I seen the day
    When praise of us was loud on every tongue,
    When never nation near our borders lay,
But sued for peace, ere peace from them was wrung.
    Great God, how close to honour's quest we clung !
Then counsellors were old, and men of action young.
Now are our rulers of such brainless breed,
To tell the end of it there's little need—
The riddle, sir, is not too hard to read.

TO THE PRINCES

YE princes, let your hearts be set on noble ends ;
    Be stark but to your foes, and gentle to your
    friends,
Aid justice, and to God give praise, by Whose consent
The wealth and lives of many in your cause are spent.
Love peace, be generous ; a good example show,
And praise of pure sweet women ye shall know ;
Hold modesty, compassion, faith, and virtue dear ;
Serve God, and to the pleadings of the poor give ear ;
Listen not to any lies ye hear,
But follow honest rede : Ye build in heaven so !

NOTE.—It may be interesting to compare this poem with the ' Envoye ' of
Chaucer's Ballade to Richard II., which is identical in tone, and curiously
similar in language :

> O Prince, desire to be honourable ;
> Cherysshe thy folke, and hate extorcioun ;
> Suffre nothing that may be reprovable
> To thyn estaate, doon in thy regioun ;
> Shew forth the swerde of castigacioun ;
> Drede God, do law, love trouthe, and worthiness ;
> And wed thy folke ageyne to stedfastnesse.

Spottiswoode & Co. Printers, New-street Square, London.

www.ingramcontent.com/pod-product-compliance
Lightning Source LLC
Chambersburg PA
CBHW030859050726
47500CB00009B/383